The Silent Partner

DIAGNOSIS MURDER

The Silent Partner

Lee Goldberg

BASED ON THE TELEVISION SERIES

CREATED BY

Joyce Burditt

THORNDIKE
CHIVERS

This Large Print edition is published by Thorndike Press®, Waterville, Maine USA and by BBC Audiobooks, Ltd, Bath, England.

Published in 2004 in the U.S. by arrangement with NAL Signet, a member of Penguin Group (USA) Inc.

Published in 2004 in the U.K. by arrangement with NAL Signet, a division of Penguin Group (USA) Inc.

U.S. Hardcover 0-7862-6169-2 (Mystery)
U.K. Hardcover 0-7540-7789-6 (Chivers Large Print)
U.K. Softcover 0-7540-7790-X (Camden Large Print)

The text of this Large Print edition is unabridged.
Other aspects of the book may vary from the original edition.

Set in 16 pt. Plantin by Al Chase.

Printed in the United States on permanent paper.

British Library Cataloguing-in-Publication Data available

Library of Congress Cataloging-in-Publication Data

Goldberg, Lee, 1962–
    The silent partner / Lee Goldberg.
        p. cm.
    "Based on the television series created by Joyce Burditt."
    ISBN 0-7862-6169-2 (lg. print : hc : alk. paper)
    1. Women — Crimes against — Fiction. 2. Medical jurisprudence — Fiction. 3. Los Angeles (Calif.) — Fiction. 4. Physicians — Fiction. 5. Large type books. I. Title: At head of title: Diagnosis murder. II. Diagnosis murder (Television program) III. Title.
    PS3557.O3577S55 2004
    813'.54—dc22   2003063983

For William Rabkin,
my partner in crime.

ACKNOWLEDGMENTS

I want to thank Dr. Doug P. Lyle for his invaluable medical advice and for letting me bombard him with all my dumb questions. Any errors are entirely my fault, which could have been avoided if I'd become a doctor like my mother wanted.

I also couldn't have written this book without the benefit of the four wonderful years I spent writing and producing *Diagnosis Murder*. My thanks to Dick Van Dyke, Barry Van Dyke, Victoria Rowell, Charlie Schlatter, Scott Baio, Michael Tucci, Kim Little, Susan Gibney, J. Larry Carroll, David Carren, Jacqueline Blain, Michael Gleason, Gerry Conway, Tom Chehak, Steve Hattman, Barry Steinberg, Fred Silverman, Dean Hargrove, Joyce Burditt, Christian Nyby, Chris Hibler, Ron Satlof, Vincent McEveety, and the rest of the crew, who made the show such a pleasure to work on, and who were in my thoughts as I wrote this book.

And, finally, a special thanks to my wife, Valerie, and my daughter, Madison, for their love and support.

PROLOGUE

In less than thirty minutes, Lydia Yates would be dead. But the twenty-three-year-old secretary didn't know that as she stood in the frozen food aisle at Ralph's Supermarket, trying to decide which equally unappealing frozen dinner, Lean Cuisine or Weight Watchers, had fewer calories. Maybe if she'd had a sneak peek at her immediate future as a corpse stuffed into a sewer pipe, she'd have spent those last few minutes of her life differently. Maybe she'd have grabbed a quart of Ben & Jerry's Chunky Monkey and gorged herself on it right there in the aisle.

The thought amused the man who would soon be killing her, though nobody would have known by looking at his face, which betrayed no emotion whatsoever. He stood at the magazine stand, flipping through a *Motor Trend* magazine, just another bored husband marking time while his wife did the shopping.

He'd picked Lydia Yates that night because she was like the others. She was the human equivalent of a generic product, the cheaper, less brightly packaged brand you buy because it costs a little less but gives you basically the same satisfaction.

The most remarkable thing about her was how truly *unremarkable* she was. She wasn't pretty enough or ugly enough to draw stares, much less a second glance. He wondered if anyone would even miss her. It might be weeks before anybody bothered to ask "Hey, whatever happened to what's her name?"

But once they found her, or what was left of her, she'd be noticed, *really* noticed. He knew Lydia Yates would be far more memorable in death than she ever was in life.

She ought to thank him for that, he thought. She ought to be picking out a nice card for him instead of trying to choose which frozen glob of toxic waste to eat.

He suppressed a smile. He was in a very good mood. A little sport always took his mind off his troubles. He wasn't nervous or even particularly excited about the murder he was going to commit. It wasn't his first, not by far, and it certainly wouldn't be the last. It was like fishing. Or bowling. Only without having to buy expensive equipment, get a license or join a league. If people knew how easy killing somebody was, and how relaxing it could be, he was sure it would really catch on.

Lydia tossed the Lean Cuisine into her cart and went to the express check-out. She was third in line. While she waited, she picked up a copy of the *Globe* and glanced at their candid photo spread on "Flabulous Celebrities." Lydia Yates spent her last three minutes as a sentient creature feeling good about herself because she'd discovered that actors have cellulite, too. If Lydia had known that her whole life would be a journey to that cosmic revelation, he wondered if she'd have welcomed the favor he was about to do for her.

She paid for her groceries and wheeled her cart out into the parking lot. It was a long walk. She'd parked her Toyota Rav4 SUV in a remote corner of the lot because she didn't want her car to get dinged.

It was a little after nine p.m. The parking lot was well lit, but mostly empty. This was an old Ralph's in an old shopping center that was going to be closed down as soon as the new Ralph's opened in the new shopping center two blocks away. The new shopping center had security cameras in the parking lot. This one didn't.

Lydia aimed her key fob remote like a ray gun and unlocked her car while she was still a good five yards away. She seemed impressed by the key fob's range. She lifted open the rear hatch, picked up her bags from the shopping cart and leaned into the car to set the groceries down. She never noticed him come up behind her.

He grabbed her jaw with one hand, the side of her head with the other, and twisted, breaking her neck and letting her dead weight carry her body into the car. He lifted up her legs, swung her body around and closed the hatch.

Fifteen seconds, a personal record.

He calmly wheeled the empty cart out of the way, waited to make sure it wouldn't roll, then went to the driver's side of Lydia's car and got in. He adjusted her seat into a comfortable driving position, started up her car and was momentarily startled by a woman's shrill voice. It was the radio. Lydia had been listening to Dr. Laura, the call-in shrink, when she'd parked.

He turned the radio off. He doubted Dr. Laura had any advice that would be helpful to Lydia now.

CHAPTER ONE

Dr. Mark Sloan, chief of internal medicine, was being paged over the Community General Hospital loudspeaker. He was wanted on the second floor right away, and he was doing his best to get there as fast as he could.

Mark rocketed down the corridors at what could only be called superhuman speed for a man of his age. He weaved around startled nurses and astonished visitors with a polite wave and a glowing smile, expertly rolling on the wheels imbedded in the heels of his Predator sneakers.

With one foot in front of the other, toes tipped up, and all his weight balanced on his heels, Mark Sloan glided down the slick linoleum floors like an Olympic ice-skater going for the Gold.

It was exhilarating for him and terrifying for everyone else. But anyone who'd visited Community General Hospital during the last forty years wouldn't have been surprised by the sight. Mark Sloan had experimented with everything from roller skates to Razor Scooters in his impossible quest to be everywhere at once.

He whipped around a corner, accidentally clipping an orderly and knocking his tray of food in the air, splattering everyone with mashed potatoes, peas and Salisbury steak. Mark looked over his shoulder to apologize and plowed into a group of candy stripers, scattering the volunteers like a flock of frightened pigeons.

That's when he saw the circular nurses' station looming up fast in front of him. Mark lowered the ball of his leading foot to the floor, going from a rapid roll into a running stop just short of a collision with the counter.

Mark smiled sheepishly at the disapproving nurse, who had thrown her considerable bulk on top of a stack of files to save them from toppling.

"I got here as fast as I could," Mark said, catching his breath.

"So I see," she said, shaking her head, each of her chins wobbling in judgment.

"Who needs a consult, Marge?" Mark asked.

"He does," Marge motioned to someone behind him.

Mark turned and was surprised to see

LAPD Police Chief John Masters leaning against the wall, his muscular arms crossed over his broad chest, staring at the doctor with his usual cold, appraising look.

The chief was a former football player who became a soldier who became a cop. He was more of a politician now than anything else, but he still carried himself like a man coiled to strike, who might be called upon at a moment's notice to tackle a quarterback, charge an enemy bunker or wrestle a deranged suspect to the ground.

"You have a unique way of getting around," Chief Masters said. His voice was low and smooth, managing to convey strength, authority and an unsettling hint of violence.

"It's called heeling," Mark lifted up one of his feet to show Masters the bottom of his shoe. "These are ordinary sneakers with removable wheels imbedded in the heels. It takes a little practice, but once you get the balance down, you can really move. You might think about it for your foot patrol officers."

"I'll be sure to do that," Masters said dismissively. "Is there somewhere private we can talk?"

"Does this have something to do with Steve?" Mark asked. Every time Steve left their Malibu beach house to go to work, pocketing his badge and strapping on his gun, Mark tried not to think about all the terrible things that could happen to him. And Mark knew from experience just how terrible those things could be.

"Doctor Sloan, if I have a problem with a homicide detective, I talk to him. I don't go running to his father."

Mark sighed with relief. "So Steve isn't hurt or in any kind of danger."

"No," the chief replied, genuinely baffled by Mark's assumption. "Why would you think that?"

"I suppose it's the natural assumption when your son is a cop and the chief of police shows up unannounced for a little talk."

"Oh, yes. Of course. I'm sorry." Masters wasn't so much sorry as he was embarrassed. He'd been so focused on his own agenda, he'd forgotten just how many times he'd done exactly what Mark described for exactly the reasons Mark feared.

"Don't worry about it, Chief," Mark said, surprising himself at how easily he was letting Masters off the hook. It was rare to see Masters flustered about anything, and Mark would ordinarily have taken advantage of it, but his curiosity was stronger than his sense of mischief.

If Masters wasn't here about Steve, what *did* he want? Some medical advice? Mark doubted it. Mark was the last person Masters would confide in about anything that could possibly be construed as revealing weakness, fear or vulnerability. Perhaps the chief finally had enough of Mark's meddling in homicide cases and had come to slap him down, once and for all.

Whatever it was, Mark would soon find out. Mark motioned Masters into one of the exam rooms and closed the door.

"So what's bothering you, Chief? One of your old football injuries acting up?"

"I'm not here for a physical, Doctor," Masters said. "I'm assembling a blue ribbon task force to do a thorough review of the department's dead case files. I want you to be on it."

The last thing Mark was expecting was any kind of job offer. "What are dead case files?"

"Unsolved homicides that are no longer being actively pursued, investigations that were reprioritized after considerable time, effort and manpower were spent on them without positive results."

It was the kind of reply Mark would have

expected to hear at a press conference. In fact, he suspected he probably would, and that the chief was simply taking it out for a test drive first.

"I think I understand," Mark said. "What you mean is these are the cases you dropped in favor of murders you knew you could close, and close quickly, to keep your annual clearance rates from dropping."

Mark gave the chief his most avuncular smile, but Masters was one of the few who was immune to it. He looked Mark in the eye and spoke very slowly, so there would be no misunderstanding. Mark tried not to wither under the big man's steely gaze.

"What I mean, Doctor, is that there are five hundred homicides in this city every year, and while we solve most of them, there are a few that we can't close. Maybe it's lack of evidence, witnesses or cooperation, or maybe it's just bad police work. I don't know. But I can tell you this: It makes me sick that those killers are still out there on the streets, making a mockery of the law. I want them behind bars. And I'm asking for your help to do it."

"Let me get this straight. You *want* me to investigate homicides. Not just any homicides, but the ones the department couldn't solve."

"I wouldn't put it that way. The mandate of the task force is to take another look at some inactive cases to see if any new leads can be developed."

"I'm confused," Mark said. "Aren't you the man who once told me 'You're a doctor, not a cop,' and wanted me thrown in jail for obstruction of justice for showing up at a crime scene? Now you're saying you *want* my help?"

The chief shifted his weight uncomfortably. He didn't like explaining himself to anyone, particularly Dr. Sloan, but he knew had no other choice.

"I don't tolerate *any* civilians getting involved in homicide investigations, particularly those lurkers, losers and lunatics who think of themselves as detectives," Masters said. "But you were regarded as some kind of expert at solving murders long before I got this job, and I can't deny you've been responsible for putting a lot of killers away, even under my watch. That said, I've never wanted your help before. This time I'm asking. That should tell you something."

It did.

So Mark decided to press his advantage and see just how much more he could get out of Masters.

"Why me?" Mark asked. "Why now?"

"I need a fresh perspective on these difficult cases and I know, for better or worse, you can give that to me."

Mark met his gaze. The chief had answered his first question but had carefully avoided the second. Mark had a pretty good idea what the answer was, and that it was the real motivation behind the blue ribbon task force and Mark's appointment to it. Even so, this was an opportunity Mark couldn't pass up, and he was well aware that Chief Masters knew it. You don't become chief of police without knowing how to skillfully manipulate people.

"When do I start?" Mark asked.

Masters reached into his jacket and handed Mark a crisply folded sheet of paper. "You already have."

As the chief walked out, Mark looked at the paper. It was an LAPD press release, dated that morning, announcing Mark's appointment to the chief's Blue Ribbon Task Force on Unsolved Homicides.

"Congratulations," Dr. Jesse Travis said, catching up to Mark in the hall.

"On what?" Mark asked.

"That whole task force thing," Jesse replied. "Very impressive."

Mark looked at the young doctor in astonishment. He'd just left Chief Masters a few minutes ago. "How did you know about it?"

"I heard it on the radio this morning," Jesse said. "Though frankly, I was a little hurt that I had to learn about it from Mike and Ken instead of you."

"I'm sure Mike and Ken, whoever they are, know more about it than I do."

"You've never listened to Mike and Ken?" Jesse said. "They're great. They once broadcast an entire show standing naked in an enormous vat of pig poop."

Mark gave him a look. "How do you know?"

"Know what?"

"That they were actually standing in pig excrement."

"They said so."

"It's radio."

Jesse thought about it a moment. "Okay, you have a point. But I know for a fact Mike can play the national anthem with his armpit."

"I'm sure it's an inspiring rendition," Mark said. "It's nice to know you're getting your news from such reliable sources."

"Hey, they knew about you and the task force, didn't they?"

Mark couldn't argue with that.

"So," Jesse said, "have you uncovered any intriguing cases?"

"I haven't looked at the files yet."

"You haven't? What are you waiting for? These cases have been buried too long already."

"I've only had the job ten minutes."

"And you're falling behind already? C'mon, Mark. I know it's hard, thankless work, but if you need help, I'm glad to lend my expertise," Jesse said. "Or just be the guy who goes out and gets the coffee and Krispy Kremes."

It wouldn't be the first time Jesse had helped Mark out on a case. Jesse was boundlessly enthusiastic, hardworking and eager to please his mentor. He reminded Mark of himself at that age, though many people, including his own son, accused Mark of intentionally molding the young doctor in his image.

Mark often wondered if Jesse really had an interest in homicide investigation or if he worked so hard at it just to please him. Solving murders wasn't actually a part of the Hippocratic Oath.

When Jesse wasn't at the hospital or helping Mark with an investigation, he could usually be found behind the counter at BBQ Bob's, a small, struggling diner he owned with Mark's son, Steve. All of this left him little time to sleep, much less do anything else, which wasn't exactly helping his relationship with his girlfriend, Susan Hilliard, a nurse at Community General. She occasionally worked the counter at BBQ Bob's just so she could spend more time with him.

"I appreciate the offer, Jesse, but it looks to me like you've got your hands full just managing your patients," Mark said, motioning to the files under Jesse's arm.

"Actually, one of them is yours." Jesse slipped one of the files out and handed it to Mark. "Stanley Tidewell checked himself in this morning."

Stanley was in his early fifties and had been one of Mark's patients, off and on, for years. He had high blood pressure, mild diabetes and a history of kidney problems. One of his kidneys had been removed several years ago and he'd been on dialysis three times a week ever since.

He was the founder of Burger Beach, a legendary, family-owned chain of local restaurants that perfectly synthesized the idealized California beach experience. Besides a simple menu of hamburgers, hot dogs, fries and shakes, Stanley's restaurants all featured suntanned waitresses in bikinis, the smell of coconut oil in the air, the sound of crashing surf piped in on hidden speakers, even a stretch of sand strewn with seashells and beach towels.

Stanley Tidewell could barely keep up with the success of his restaurants, opening new locations as fast as he could, regularly putting in twenty-hour days and eating off his own menu. He refused to slow down or change his lifestyle, despite Mark's dire warnings about the risks he was taking with his health.

Mark treated him for a kidney infection a couple of months ago, but other than that, Stanley's condition had remained remarkably stable. At least until now.

"I'm getting him dialysized, running the usual tests and keeping a close eye on his electrolytes," Jesse said. "You don't need to worry, I'm on top of it."

"What's his problem?" Mark asked. "Did his kidney infection come back?"

"No. He's fine."

"Then what's he doing in the hospital?"

"Mr. Tidewell decided to have a kidney transplant. He's found a private donor and he's flying in some big shot surgeon to do the operation," Jesse said. "I thought you knew all about it."

Mark shook his head and handed the file back. "I guess I better start listening to *Mike & Ken* or I'm never going to know anything."

Mark glanced down the hall as the elevator arrived and people began filing out. He couldn't see anybody waiting to get in, which meant in a moment the doors would close on an empty elevator. He narrowed his eyes and calculated the variables.

"I'll catch up with you later," Mark said.

And with that, Mark ran a few steps, lifted the balls of his feet, shifted his weight to his heels and rocketed towards the empty elevator, making it inside with a triumphant smile just as the elevator doors were closing. There was, however, one variable Mark hadn't considered — how he was going to stop.

An instant later, Jesse heard a heavy *thunk* and a muffled *"yee-ouch!"* from inside the elevator.

Jesse couldn't figure out how such a brilliant man could also be such an incredible klutz. There had to be a balance there somewhere, but Jesse couldn't find it. He'd seen many people judge Mark Sloan by his eccentricities and underestimate his genius. That was a big mistake, one Jesse never made. Instead, he respected Mark's intelligence, learned from his example as a doctor and, as he had that afternoon, simply accepted his odd behavior for what it was. Odd.

The young doctor took one more look at the elevator, grinned to himself and happily continued on his rounds.

CHAPTER TWO

Jesse walked into Stanley Tidewell's hospital room and was stunned by what he saw.

The room had been transformed into an office complete with fax machines, computers and two staffers chattering on their cell phones. The framed, manufactured prints of bland seascapes and fruit bowls were on the floor, replaced by restaurant blueprints and detailed maps of Southern California. The neighborhood maps were covered with multicolored pins representing current Burger Beach outlets and new locations.

Stanley Tidewell was sitting on top of the bed in an exercise suit, one sleeve rolled up while Jesse's girlfriend, Susan Hilliard, RN, finished taking his blood for what the patient lamented was "the umpteenth time."

Let him lament, Jesse thought. The doctor wanted to be absolutely sure there was nothing wrong with Stanley that might jeopardize the surgery or prompt rejection of the new kidney. He'd already checked Stanley out for infections and viruses and questioned him about any allergies. So far, his blood was clean, and his allergies to high-SPF sunscreen, penicillin and flea-bites wouldn't be a problem. It was the office stress Stanley had literally brought with him into the hospital, not to mention the sack of hamburgers and fries on the nightstand, that concerned Jesse now.

"Mr. Tidewell," Jesse said. "What do you think you're doing?"

"Taking care of a little business, that's all." Stanley was the kind of heavyset guy people thought of as jolly instead of fat because of his rosy cheeks, sparkling eyes and almost permanent smile. "It's more productive than sitting in bed reading magazines and watching Oprah."

"You're not supposed to be productive in a hospital bed; you're supposed to be resting up. You need to get rid of all this stuff and get these people out of here."

"This is my son, Billy." Stanley motioned to one of the people Jesse had assumed were part of Tidewell's secretarial staff. Billy looked like a taller, tanner, fitter version of his father. "He's my right hand and my kidney, too."

"He's your donor?"

"He's checking himself in tomorrow," Stanley said. "So, you can see, with both of us out of commission for a while, how important it is we get as much work done before the operation as possible. We're opening three restaurants this month. Next year we're going national."

"Is Billy aware of the risks involved in donating his kidney?"

"Billy is." Billy snapped his cell phone shut and approached Jesse. "My father's kidney disease isn't genetic. I'm in terrific health. I run three miles every morning. I don't smoke, drink or do any drugs. I can easily live on one kidney, so the least I can do is save my dad's life by giving him my spare."

"It's not a spare, and your dad's life isn't in any jeopardy right now. This is elective surgery." Jesse turned to Stanley. "The truth is, Mr. Tidewell, you may never need a transplant if you make some simple adjustments in your lifestyle."

"Why should I? It's obviously working for me. Look how rich and happy I am. The only change I want to make is to stop going into the clinic three times a week for dialysis. We're a small, family-run business. It's just me and Billy. I can't afford to be wasting so much time."

"You're keeping yourself alive; that's hardly a waste of time."

"My God, you sound just like Mark Sloan," Stanley said with a grin.

"I learned from the best." Jesse shared a smile with Susan. She knew how much he admired Mark and what a compliment Stanley had unknowingly given him.

"Frankly, Doc, dialysis is a chore and I'm tired of it. One simple operation and I'll never have to do it again."

"No surgery is risk free, Mr. Tidewell. There is really no reason to be gambling with your son's health right now."

"I enjoy gambling, but this hardly qualifies," Billy replied. "Doctors do twelve thousand kidney transplants a year. Donors rarely suffer even mild complications. And less than half the kidney recipients experience organ rejection, and even that can usually be controlled with drugs. The odds are very much on our side."

"I appreciate your concern, Doc," Stanley said, "but we've thought it all out, we've done our research and we've hired the top surgeon in the field. A couple days from now, I'll be a new man."

Jesse could think of a hundred more arguments, but he knew it was pointless. Stanley's mind was made up, and nothing he said was going to change it.

Stanley Tidewell wasn't in dire need of a new kidney. He wasn't in any danger of renal failure yet. He didn't need this operation. But Jesse wondered how much of his opposition was actually based on jealousy instead of medical judgment.

He could see that Stanley and his son Billy were obviously very close. They were in business together. They probably saw each other every day. Billy thought nothing of ripping out one of his kidneys just to make his dad's life a little easier.

Jesse had no doubt Steve would do the same thing for Mark without blinking. But Jesse knew he'd hesitate before doing the same for his own father. It wasn't that he didn't love him; he just hardly knew him. His parents divorced when he was young, mostly because his dad was never around and even when he was, kept mostly to himself.

Jesse longed for the father-son relationship that seemed to come so easily, and so naturally, to Mark and Steve, Stanley and Billy and every other father and son except for Dane and Jesse Travis. He often thought about whether he'd gravitated towards Mark and gone into business with Steve to get closer to what he didn't have and probably never would.

So, was that really his problem with this operation? That Stanley had such a great relationship with his son? What was so wrong with a son wanting to make life better for his dad?

"I'm sure you will be fine, Mr. Tidewell," Jesse said. "And I apologize if I came across too strong. I just wanted to be certain you were both making an informed decision. It sounds to me like you are. Have your surgeon come see me as soon as he gets in."

"Will do, Doc."

Jesse turned to Billy. "We're going to need to start running some blood work on you today, to screen for any infections, viruses or compatibility problems."

"Whatever you need."

Jesse nodded his head towards Susan. "Nurse Hilliard will get on it right after you turn this office back into a hospital room."

"Is that really necessary?" Stanley asked.

"It is if you're serious about this operation." Jesse snatched the Burger Beach take-out bag off the nightstand and lobbed it into the trash. "And no more junk food."

"It tastes a lot better than the slop you serve here," Stanley said with a smile.

"Maybe I ought to talk to the hospital about taking over your food services — turn the cafeteria into a Burger Beach franchise. I bet your patients would be a lot happier."

Stanley meant it as a joke, but as he was saying it, suddenly the idea sounded pretty good to him. "Billy, we ought to look into that. You realize how many hospitals there are in the country? They've got a strong, and captive, customer base and we'd only be looking at half the building costs of a typical outlet. It's cheaper than going into a mall or an airport, and the hospitals might be so eager to give up the headaches of running restaurants that they'll kick in some cash to cover our start-up costs."

"That's a great idea, Dad." Billy started jotting some notes on a legal pad. "I'll get you some figures to think about."

That's when Jesse's attention was drawn to the map of Burger Beach outlets and new locations. He stepped up to it, scrutinized the pins and tried to hide his surprise at what he saw.

"You're putting in a Burger Beach across the street from BBQ Bob's?" Jesse asked. "Aren't you worried about the competition?"

"From that place?" Stanley waved off the

suggestion. "I doubt it will last ninety days after we open."

Susan shot Jesse a worried look, but Jesse kept a poker face.

"I wouldn't be so sure about that," Jesse offered casually. "The ribs are awfully good, the service is great and the customers are very loyal."

"The only reason that place is still in business is because there's no other place on the block to eat. They are barely hanging on. We're an established chain with deep pockets and an advertising budget. They can barely afford napkins. If we only take a quarter of their business, they'll have to close down."

"I think you're underestimating how popular BBQ Bob's is. The place has real charm."

"A babe in a bikini beats charm any day."

Jesse forced a weak smile, said his good-byes and left the room. Susan caught up with him in the hall.

"Why don't you tell him," she asked.

"Tell him what?"

"That you own BBQ Bob's. Maybe he'll reconsider and open his restaurant somewhere else."

"Susan, he's running a business and you

can see how serious he is about it. He's not going to drop everything because one of his doctors invested in the dive across the street."

"You don't know unless you ask."

"I got a better idea."

"What's that?"

"You ever tried waitressing in a bikini?"

She tried to swat him, but he'd already dashed out of range.

The only sound in Mark Sloan's beach house was the mingling of the crashing surf with the tidelike passing of late-night traffic on the Pacific Coast Highway.

Mark sat hunched over his laptop at the kitchen table, facing the tall windows and the large deck that overlooked the beach. The windows were open, the salty, slightly fishy scent of the ocean mist riding on the gentle breeze that wafted through the house. He looked up from his screen, took a deep breath and let it out slowly.

He loved living there, yet it was a pleasure mixed with a measure of guilt. His late wife Katherine loved the beach. They often dreamed of having a beach house some day, after their children were raised, his responsibilities at the hospital tapered off and they had plenty of time for each other. But she never envisioned that Mark's casual interest in homicide investigation would ultimately become so consuming or that their son would follow in his grandfather's footsteps and become a cop.

For most of their marriage, they lived in a sprawling, ranch style house in Brentwood, and after Katherine died, he'd stayed there for many years. But the crush of memories finally became too much, extending his sorrow and deepening his pain. Mark knew he had to leave.

And so there he was, with a house right on the beach, living the dream he never got to share with his wife. Sharing the house with Steve took the edge off his guilt but never quite erased it.

The two-story house was far too big for just one person, or even two really, but the extra space allowed Mark and Steve to live together and yet still have separate lives.

The top floor was the main area of the house, and Mark's home, with three bedrooms, a gourmet kitchen and a huge living room dominated by a massive stone fireplace and high, wood-beam ceiling. The shelves on either side of the fireplace were filled with books, antique medical equipment, bits and pieces of old magic tricks and knickknacks gathered on his travels. A comfortable, well-worn leather couch and matching armchairs were angled so he could enjoy the warmth of the fireplace and the view of the beach.

A winding staircase in the entry hall led down to the first floor, where Steve lived. The first floor had a separate kitchen, a full bath and a big bedroom that opened directly onto the beach. It also had a private entrance, which Steve only used when he brought home a date. He wasn't sneaking around. He was being practical. It wasn't easy for a homicide detective to get a date. It got exponentially harder when women found out he still lived with his father.

Mark occasionally wondered whether it was a special bond between him and his son that kept Steve there, or if it was simply the prime beach front real estate. But Mark didn't really care what the reasons were. He considered himself the luckiest father in the world.

He heard Steve coming in the front door and called out to him from the kitchen. Steve ambled in, looking very tired, and unclipped the gun from his belt and set it on the counter.

"There's leftover chicken in the fridge if you're interested," Mark said.

"Thanks." Steve went to the refrigerator, pulled out the plate of chicken and grabbed a bottle of beer.

"Tough case?" Mark asked.

"Not really. Just pointless and depressing," Steve said, twisting the cap off the beer and taking a sip. "A couple gang members decide to catch a movie, which to them means paying eight bucks to sit in the front row and yell lewd remarks at Jennifer Lopez. So that's how it goes. The movie starts and they're yelling at the screen. It's dark; they're way up front; nobody knows these loudmouths are gang members. Some guy in the back shouts at them to pipe down, so naturally they pull out their semiautomatic guns and shoot him a dozen times."

Steve took a few bites from a chicken leg. "I'm not exactly dealing with criminal masterminds. Most of my cases can be closed in forty-eight hours or less. You won't find many of them among the files you'll be looking at."

"So you heard about the task force on the department grapevine."

"No, from Mike and Ken," Steve said.

"Don't tell me you listen to those guys, too," Mark said. "They sit in a giant bucket of excrement."

"Apparently the experience has given them a much better understanding of L.A. politics than you have," Steve said. "They see the chief's 'Blue Ribbon' task force for what it really is."

"It's a blatant political move to generate some positive publicity for himself before he announces his candidacy for Mayor."

"Then you know he doesn't really expect the task force to accomplish anything," Steve said. "It's just a show. He's using you to deflect attention away from the city's rising crime rate. He wants voters to think he's so tough on crime that he's unwilling to turn his back even on open homicides that have been dormant for decades."

"You're probably right, but I don't have anything to lose except my time, and if a fresh look at the files leads to just one new clue emerging in an unsolved murder, then it will be worth it."

"Dad, this is a rigged game. There's a reason those cases are inactive. Either they were dead ends to start with, or they've already been worked from every possible angle. If you guys fail, Masters still comes across as tough on crime and the department is off the hook. It will be you and the task force that looks bad, which is exactly what he wants."

"That's a chance I'm willing to take," Mark said. "Regardless of what the chief's motivations are for creating the task force, we're the last hope the families of all those forgotten murder victims have of finally seeing some justice done."

"But you lose either way. If you actually solve one of those inactive cases, the department will look inept. The chief can't let that happen, so he'll do whatever he can to stall your progress and discredit the task force."

Mark shrugged. "So be it."

Steve scraped his chicken bones into the trash, put his plate in the sink and picked up his beer. "I admire your principles, Dad. But principles and politics just don't mix, not in L.A. anyway."

Steve motioned with his bottle to the laptop. "What are you working on so late?"

"Researching the origins of the phrase 'Blue Ribbon.'"

"You've got to be kidding."

"People are always calling panels and commissions and task forces 'blue ribbon,' as if that confers on them special power. So I got curious. What does it really mean?" Mark tapped a few keys on his laptop, bringing up a screenful of text and pictures of all kinds of blue ribbons. "At first, I thought it might have something to do with the ribbons you win at the County Fair. Well, it actually goes back to the Middle Ages as a way of distinguishing warriors on the battlefield. Various colored ribbons were used to display coats of arms. Later the blue ribbon itself became recognized as the highest point of honor attainable in a given profession. The cordon bleu, for example, is descended from —"

Mark turned to look at Steve only to discover that he was gone. He shrugged and turned back to the information on his laptop. There probably wasn't any reason he'd ever need to know the history of the blue ribbon. But Mark believed you never knew when a little useless knowledge might suddenly prove useful.

CHAPTER THREE

The world's largest thermometer, a neon and cement monolith, rose 135 feet over Baker, California, a patch of sun-bleached gas stations, coffee shops and decrepit motels off Interstate 15, right smack in the center of the sweltering Mojave Desert.

It was ten o'clock at night and, according to the world's largest thermometer, it was 102 degrees outside. A sign beneath the cheesy landmark proclaimed that Baker was the "Gateway to Death Valley." Scratch out the word valley and the sign would accurately describe what the place was about to become for Jerry Ridling, the young hitchhiker sitting on the curb, sucking down a strawberry milk shake.

The hitchhiker obviously hadn't been on the road long. He had about a week's growth of stubble on his sunburned face. His hair was unwashed but recently cut. His clothes were wrinkled but clean. It would have been obvious to anybody that his dirty backpack and bedroll were brand-new even if the dumb kid had remembered to cut the sales tag off the shoulder strap. This was a nineteen-year-old out on an adventure, a kid who thought it might be fun and romantic and just a little scary to hitchhike from wherever to wherever before going to college or getting married or working for his daddy. Something to talk about on first dates. Something to tell his kids about someday to prove he wasn't the boring guy they thought he was. Something to use as inspiration for his novel, if he ever decided to write one.

The killer had been waiting for Jerry, or someone like him, for a couple hours now. The killer was patient. He knew it was only a matter of time. Even on a weeknight like this, there was a steady stream of cars and trucks passing by on the interstate. Every few minutes somebody would take the off-ramp to fill up their tank or empty their bladder on their way to or from someplace else. Nobody came here to be here. Most of the northeast traffic was headed for Las Vegas, ninety miles away. The rest were probably going to L.A.

He'd watched the hitchhiker get out of a pickup truck with a camper shell that was dragging a couple dirt bikes on a trailer. They were clearly going to the desert for some off-roading and probably agreed to take Jerry as far as Baker, assuring the kid that he'd have

43

no problem getting a ride the rest of the way to Vegas.

The hitchhiker watched the pickup drive off, craned his head up at the world's largest thermometer, then looked around the dusty street. Being a man of adventure, Jerry ignored the franchises like Denny's and Burger King and sought out local color. He was immediately drawn to The Mad Greek, a blue-and-white-striped monstrosity with drooping American flags on every corner of its roof and garish banners along its awnings offering "world famous strawberry shakes," as well as waffles, hamburgers, baklava and donut holes.

The hitchhiker went in and a few moments later came out with his shake. Being a seasoned world traveler, naturally he chose to sample their "world famous" specialty over their fish and chips and kourambiethes. Jerry walked a hundred yards to stretch his legs and sat down on a curb, far from the nearest flickering streetlight. Behind him were four dreary palm trees and the abandoned, decrepit hulk of the Royal Tiki Palms Motel, its faded sign still promising "clean restrooms" and "thermometer views." Dry weeds poked through the cracked asphalt of the parking lot. The empty pool was a cement pit filled with fast food trash and rusty lawn furniture.

The killer waited for Jerry to finish his

shake, then approached him from the darkness, startling him with a hearty and friendly hello. He asked the kid if he needed a ride. The kid, so pleased not to have to wag his thumb on the road again, quickly said yes, he did, and asked where the man was heading.

Las Vegas, the killer said. I have a shipment of mattresses to deliver to one of the big casinos.

Great, the kid said. That's exactly where I'm heading.

The killer said his rig was parked on the other side of the hotel. As they started to walk, the killer asked Jerry where he was from and what his travels had been like. It was like turning on a spigot. The kid couldn't stop talking, so pleased and eager to share his dull little adventures. Jerry was so busy talking, he didn't notice just how far off the main road they were walking or ask himself why a truck driver would park his rig behind a deserted motel or why a guy would be wearing leather gloves when it was over a hundred degrees outside. And when some part of his subconscious finally sensed that something was wrong and rang the panic alarm loud enough for the kid to hear through the noise of his own chatter, it was far too late.

Jerry stopped talking, and walking, midsentence. It took him a second to realize that there was nothing but empty desert in front of him and what that might mean. He turned to run but didn't get more than two steps before the killer grabbed him by the strap of his backpack, spun him around and drove the ice pick deep into his stomach. Once. Twice. Three times.

Still holding him by the straps of his backpack, the killer dragged Jerry's twitching body to the edge of the pool and, with the toe of his boot, tipped him over the side.

Steve stopped in for breakfast at BBQ Bob's on his way in to work and was startled to see the waitresses in shorts and halter tops. The mostly male customers didn't seem to mind, but the waitresses didn't look too pleased about it. He spotted Jesse in the kitchen and waved him over.

"What's going on?" Steve asked.

"What do you mean?"

Steve glanced at one of the waitresses. She was leaning down, setting a plate of bacon and eggs in front of a truck driver who almost tipped out of his seat trying to keep his eyes on her cleavage.

"I feel like I've walked into a strip joint," Steve said.

"That's great!"

"Jesse, pretty soon the guys in here are going to start sticking dollar bills in the waitresses' skirts."

"And that's a bad thing?"

"Yes, it's a bad thing."

"Do you want to stay in business or not?"

"I want to stay in the *restaurant* business. I'm not ready to branch out into adult entertainment," Steve said, glancing at the waitresses again. "Why are they dressed like that?"

"That's our new uniform."

"That's not a uniform. My tie covers more skin."

"Fine, they can wear ties instead."

"I think you're missing my point."

The bell above the front door jangled, signaling the arrival of a new customer. It was Dr. Amanda Bentley, wearing her official, navy blue windbreaker with the words MEDICAL EXAMINER emblazoned in big yellow letters on the back.

The African-American woman had multitasking down to an art. Somehow Amanda managed to juggle being the divorced parent of a five-year-old boy with the taxing responsibilities of being both chief pathologist at Community General and an adjunct county medical examiner.

It wasn't as if she needed the money. The interest on her trust fund could probably support five families. She took on the two jobs because she loved the work.

"I thought I'd find you here," she said to Steve, taking a seat beside him at the counter. "We got a floater waiting for us in Balona Creek. Badly decomposed, probably been in the water a week."

"Lower your voice, please," Jesse said, then nodded at her windbreaker. "And do you have to wear that in here? It's bad for business."

She glanced at the waitresses, then back to Jesse. "Maybe you'd be happier if I was in my underwear."

"We were just talking about that," Steve said.

"About me in my underwear?" Amanda asked.

"About our half-naked waitresses." Steve turned back to Jesse. "I need two strong coffees to go and an explanation."

Jesse poured the coffees into two tall Styrofoam cups. "I just found out they're opening a Burger Beach across the street."

Steve groaned and massaged his temples. It was moments like this when he asked himself what the hell he was thinking, getting into the restaurant business. That was

48

just it. He *didn't* think. Not for a second.

BBQ Bob's had always been one of his favorite places to eat. One day he came in for lunch and discovered that Bob was retiring, closing the place down and taking his incredible secret recipe for the preparation of barbecue spareribs with him. Steve couldn't stand the thought of losing those ribs.

So, on a whim, a crazy, lunatic whim, he went to Jesse, who loved the ribs as much as he did, and suggested they buy the place. Jesse instantly agreed. Of course, neither one of them could afford it, not on a cop's and a third year resident's salaries, so they had to beg Mark for a loan, making him a silent partner and a constant moocher of free food.

But they did it. BBQ Bob's was theirs.

Now everybody thought he used hickory smoke for cologne. Now all his clothes were covered with barbecue stains. Now time he could have spent surfing or dirt biking or just sleeping in was spent bussing tables, doing dishes, cleaning bathrooms and paying bills.

What was he *thinking?*

And yet, he didn't want to lose it. Not to Burger Beach or anything else. BBQ Bob's was his oasis. A place where he could forget the horrors he saw on the job. Something that was his, and his alone.

Okay, his and Jesse's, and theirs alone, but the feeling was the same.

There was also the barbecue recipe to consider. That incredible combination of sauce and smoke and spices and passion. It was a barbecue masterpiece, a culinary work of art, and he had an obligation to protect it for the good of mankind.

Suddenly, the new uniforms weren't looking so bad.

Amanda looked at Steve and seemed to read his thoughts.

"You can't win against Burger Beach by competing with their" — she looked at the waitress as she searched for the right word — "decor. You'll just have to rely on your good food and friendly service."

"We're finished," Jesse said grimly.

"Don't be so sure," Amanda said. "You've also got plenty of charm."

"I know that," Jesse replied. "I'm just trying to show off some of it."

Amanda gave him the scolding look she usually reserved for Colin, her five-year-old.

"She's right, Jesse." Steve sighed and rose from his stool. "Give them back their old uniforms before we get raided by the vice squad."

Steve and Amanda took their coffees and headed out the door to a new day, and a new corpse, just as Susan was coming in. The look of horror, and then fury, on her face spelled doom for Jesse. He closed his eyes and slowly slid under the counter. Some days it just didn't pay to get up in the morning.

A tangle of water pipes, air ducts, electrical conduits, computer cables and telephone lines snaked like intertwined vines along the walls and ceiling of the subbasement deep below Parker Center, the headquarters of the Los Angeles Police Department.

Mark Sloan's steps echoed down the long, empty corridor, which was lit by an unevenly spaced line of lightbulbs, each encased in some sort of industrial-looking wire cage, as if they were live animals that might escape.

The only sound besides his footsteps was a constant electric hum that came either from the imprisoned bulbs or some unseen device behind one of the unmarked, gray doors.

The air was still, humid and dusty. Trapped, just like the lightbulbs. Trapped, just like Mark.

He fought a sudden urge to turn around and run. That's when he came to a door marked D-127. He checked the number against the one written on the slip of paper crumpled in his hand. This was the right place.

Mark opened the door and walked into a cramped room, hundreds of cardboard cartons stacked haphazardly from floor to ceiling against the cement walls. In the center of the room, under one jailed lightbulb, was a wobbly card table and four folding chairs. Sitting in one of those chairs, stubbing out a cigarette onto the vinyl table top, was a familiar face.

"Welcome to the Command Center for the Blue Ribbon Task Force on Unsolved Homicides," Lt. Tanis Archer said. "I hope you brought a bucket and some towels. There's not much in the way of amenities down here."

Mark walked slowly around the room and was shocked to discover the stack of boxes was actually two rows deep. He wondered how many cases there were in each box and how many years back the boxes went. His gaze drifted over the handwritten labels on some of them: "Oct–Dec 1971," "R. Demming Homicide — 1957, Box 1 of 3," "April–June, A–C, 1999,"

"John Does 1–17, 1986." There didn't seem to be any kind of organizing principle behind how the boxes were stacked beyond dumping them where they wouldn't be seen, where they wouldn't be constant reminders of work undone.

The enormity of what he'd volunteered to do was beginning to sink in.

"Have the files always been here," he asked, "or did the chief move them down for our benefit?"

"You can add that to our list of mysteries to solve."

Mark slid out a chair and sat down. He already felt exhausted, and they hadn't even started work yet. He glanced at Tanis. "So is the task force just the two of us?"

"The panel is comprised of three civilian experts in the field of homicide investigation and an official liaison with the department, which would be me," Tanis said, jerking a thumb at herself.

Mark Sloan and Tanis Archer had only worked together a few times, but he'd been impressed by her tenacity, her toughness and her single-minded determination to see cases through to the end. She had a healthy respect for authority, as long as authority stayed the hell out of her way.

She'd worked undercover. She'd worked

gangs. She'd worked sex crimes. And she'd worked homicide. But the one thing she'd never worked was a desk or, for that matter, a card table.

"Why are you the liaison?" Mark asked.

"Because I caught a guy beating up his girlfriend, and when he resisted arrest, I gave him the opportunity to personally experience what it was like to be her," Tanis said, a satisfied smile on her face. She was proud of beating the guy up, even if she might have exceeded her authority and the boundaries of acceptable police conduct herself.

"You were accused of using excessive force," Mark said.

"No, that wasn't the problem. Nobody, not even the perp, says I threw one more punch than was necessary to put him down," she said. "The problem was the perp was the son of a deputy police chief. I was asked to lose the paperwork, to let him off with a warning. For whipping a woman with a garden hose? For taking a swing at a police officer? No way. I wouldn't do it. I put his ass in jail and sent the case to the DA. Word got out; the press got on it; there were some negative stories in the paper. They *had* to prosecute him after that, or look like they were giving a deputy chief special treatment. I embarrassed the department, not that anyone actually told me that. Instead, I was appointed to the Blue Ribbon Task Force on Unsolved Homicides."

"I see," Mark said.

To people outside the department, her appointment would certainly be seen as a promotion, a sign of respect. That way, no one could accuse Masters of retaliating against her for arresting the deputy chief's son. But within the department, the reassignment would be seen for what it was. A demotion. And a clear warning from Masters to the rank and file about the price that would be paid for defying authority.

Though Mark truly sympathized with her plight, he was glad to have her on the task force. If she hadn't conveniently screwed up when she did, the chief probably would have assigned them some deadbeat cop who was just biding his time until retirement. She wouldn't have wanted to hear that, so instead Mark tried to change the subject.

"Now that you're on the task force," Mark said jovially, "perhaps you'd like to know the significance of the blue ribbon."

"I'd rather slam my head against the wall

a few times and see if you could revive me."

Mark was spared having to prove his ability to treat serious head trauma by the arrival of two men, neither of whom he'd ever met, but both of whom he recognized. They were Lou Rozan and Freddy Meeks.

Lou Rozan was a quiet man in his early forties with intense blue eyes, buzz-cut blond hair and a chiseled physique sculpted by hours at the gym. He was considered one of the FBI's best profilers. For years, he'd been on call 24/7, crisscrossing the country from one grisly, unspeakably horrific homicide scene to another. The job was Lou's life until a year ago, when he reportedly suffered a mild breakdown while chasing a serial killer who preyed on young children. A short time later, Lou left the FBI and went into the private sector, becoming a consultant to a number of high-end, private security firms.

Mark was surprised Lou Rozan agreed to join the task force and wondered if perhaps this was the profiler's first tentative step towards returning to an active role in law enforcement.

Freddy Meeks always looked like he'd just crawled out of bed. His brown hair was perpetually tousled, he always had at least a day's growth of beard on his face and his clothes were usually wrinkled. But Freddy got away with it, thanks to his easy, boyish grin and a mischievous sparkle in his eyes that never seemed to dim.

His appearance, which Mark often thought was too consistent to be anything but premeditated, was in sharp contrast to his occupation. Meeks was an ex–*Los Angeles Times* crime beat reporter who'd become the bestselling author of a string of "true crime" books about serial killers. Mark had read, and admired, just about every one of them, for the same reasons the critics did. Meeks' books read like novels, earning him favorable comparisons to Norman Mailer and Truman Capote for his uncanny ability to "get inside the heads" of the psychopathic killers, the victims and the cops he wrote about. His books were based on interviews, court documents and his astonishing network of unnamed sources within the law enforcement community — and it was widely believed that Lou Rozan was one of them.

The one thing that troubled Mark about Meeks' books was how much the serial killers he wrote about enjoyed the attention. Now it was frighteningly common for killers to send Meeks fan notes from death row, asking him to write about their cases and give them some measure of immortality.

As soon as Lou and Freddy came in the room, greetings and introductions were made all around and the two men joined Mark and Tanis at the table. Lou stowed a neon blue, polyethylene lunchbox under his chair. Obviously, Lou came prepared. Mark could see this wasn't the first task force he'd worked on and probably wouldn't be the last.

"Before we get started, I've got a confession to make," Freddy flashed his boyish, bemused smile. "I'm only here to get a peek at the Black Dahlia file, and then I'm gone."

The Black Dahlia case was perhaps the most notorious unsolved murder in L.A. history. In 1947, the dismembered corpse of a twenty-two-year-old woman named Elizabeth Short was found in a vacant lot. The corpse had been washed and drained of blood, her black hair died red, and there were signs that she'd been tied and beaten before her gruesome death. The case was never solved but became the subject of countless movies and books.

"I'm afraid the cases we're going to see will be a lot less sensational or they wouldn't be down here," Lou said. "So if you got into this looking for your next book, you're in for a big disappointment."

Freddy shook his head in mock dismay. "Does that mean we aren't going to find out who really killed Thelma Todd, George Reeves or Bugsy Siegel either?"

Tanis Archer grunted. "We'll be lucky if we can figure out the *name* of just one of the 318 unidentified homicide victims the city had to bury in unmarked graves."

They were all silent for a moment, listening to the omnipresent electric hum, mentally preparing themselves for the laborious task ahead.

"How shall we proceed?" Mark asked, offering the question to the room.

Tanis stood up, lifted the nearest box, and dropped it in the center of the card table, which nearly collapsed under the sudden weight.

"They're all the same," she said. "They're all dead. We might as well just open up a box and get started."

CHAPTER FOUR

Without meaning to, Mark and the others stumbled into a procedure for sorting through the files. Each of them plucked a file out of the box, scanned the details, and then summarized the case for the others. They discussed each case and then whether they thought there was more work that could be done on it.

They broke for a late afternoon lunch without finding a single unsolved homicide that hadn't already been investigated as far as it could go. They continued to work while they ate, Lou eating his fruits, vegetables and some kind of shake, while the others shared a cold Domino's pizza. It took the poor delivery guy an hour to find their basement office.

Mark was very disappointed by their progress or, rather, their lack of it. Despite his conversation with Steve, he really felt he'd be able to find many cases that could be reopened. And not because the original cops did it wrong the first time. He'd have the benefit of examining the homicides from a totally different perspective. He would be free from the stress of working several different homicides at once, from the departmental pressure to clear cases quickly, and from the heart-wrenching pleas of grieving family members demanding swift justice. He'd also be coming at these murders unfettered by previous investigative assumptions and an overfamiliarity with the details.

Mark had convinced himself he'd discover clues that went unnoticed, witness accounts that didn't correspond with the facts or forensic evidence open to reinterpretation. Instead, after six long hours, it became clear to Mark, and to his colleagues on the task force, that most of these cases were hopeless from the start.

There were the unidentified corpses. A headless, fingerless body in the Angeles National Forest. The man weighed down with rocks under a Marina Del Rey boat dock. The decapitated head in a Dumpster. The woman set aflame in a Van Nuys alley. The body in a motel bathtub full of lye.

There were the gang murders. Countless drive-by shootings in which dozens of gang members were assassinated and even more innocent bystanders were killed, the investigations hobbled by the unwillingness of a single witness to come forward.

And there were the killings that defied easy categorization. The commuter found stabbed to death in his parked car on a freeway shoulder. The family massacred in their home. The shipping container found on a San Pedro dock, the corpses of a dozen illegal immigrants locked inside.

So much death. So little to go on. And this was only the first day.

Lou closed the file he'd just taken from the box and handed it back to Tanis without summarizing it for the others. "This one is misfiled."

"Can't be. There is no filing system." She slid the file back across the table to him. "At least not that I can see."

"What I mean is this case was solved," Lou said. "The file shouldn't be in this room."

The peculiarity of the mistake was the first thing that managed to grab Mark's interest all morning. How did a closed homicide end up among the inactive, unsolved murders? Out of curiosity, he picked up the file and scanned through it.

It concerned the murder of Lydia Yates, a twenty-two-year-old temporary secretary who disappeared from a Ralph's grocery store parking lot in Simi Valley three years ago. Her corpse was found days later, stuffed inside a sewer pipe a few miles away in Moorpark, her neck broken. For some reason, the victim and the circumstances of her murder seemed familiar to Mark.

Lou watched Mark browsing through the file. "You're wasting your time, Mark; we know who killed her."

"We do?" Tanis asked.

"She was one of the victims of a serial killer known as the Reaper," Lou replied.

"I thought the details sounded familiar." Mark looked at Freddy. "Didn't I read your book about it?"

"I hope so. Every sale helps me make the lease payments on my Ferrari," Freddy said. "I only wrote about the Reaper; Lou actually helped catch him."

"So how come I don't have the Ferrari?" Lou said. "I came into it after the third victim was discovered. They were all single women, average looking, a little lonely. They were last seen doing some routine, domestic chore. Going to the Laundromat. Getting a car wash. Picking up a prescription at the drugstore. Getting a cheeseburger. And they were all killed the same way. Approached from behind, their necks broken. I didn't have a hard time working up a profile."

"He's killing women because he's been dominated by them all his life," Freddy said by rote. "He chooses weak women and approaches them from behind because, as much as he hates them, he also fears them. He's in his early thirties, about six feet tall and 170 pounds."

Mark nodded at Lou, impressed. "You deduced his physical characteristics from the height of the victims and the physical force it would take to break their necks."

Lou shrugged. "That was the easy part. The final profile was a lot more detailed than that, particularly from a psychological viewpoint. We honed it as more victims were discovered and we could make more educated assumptions."

An education that relied on lessons learned from an ever increasing number of victims, Mark thought. It was a tragic fact.

"How did you catch him?" Tanis asked.

"Read the book and find out," Freddy said. "I'll even autograph it for you."

"I'll save you twenty-five bucks," Lou said. "We were able to narrow down the general area where the Reaper liked to hunt and how often he liked to do it. We put several grocery stores, Laundromats, fast food joints and car washes under surveillance and sent in undercover agents who matched the specs of his victims. Then we waited for guys who matched the profile. We got lucky. He walked into one of our stings, followed an undercover cop to her car and tried to break her neck. She broke his wrist in three places instead."

While Lou explained the details to Tanis, Mark continued to peruse the file. The paperwork didn't appear to match up with Lou's account of the facts.

"You say Lydia Yates was one of the Reaper's victims, but I don't see anything in this file indicating that you won a conviction." Mark flipped through the file, looking for the documents.

Lou shifted uncomfortably in his seat. "That's because we didn't."

"You've lost me," Mark said. "I thought you said the case was closed."

"The Reaper killed nine women, but we were only able to prove six of the cases. We know he murdered the others, but he wouldn't confess to them and we didn't have enough to make the cases in court."

"So her homicide *isn't* closed," Mark said.

"The Reaper killed the other three

women," Lou said emphatically. "The evidence at the scenes matched details of the previous homicides that were never released to the media. So, while *technically* the Yates case is unsolved, we do know who killed her."

"Then I think you should have been able to prove it." Mark turned to Tanis. "I'd like to see the files on the other two victims whose murders were attributed to the Reaper but never proven."

Lou groaned wearily. "Mark, we have hundreds of cases here that aren't solved. We know who did this one. He's on death row. Let's move on."

"I agree with Lou," Tanis said to Mark. "This is pointless."

"I'd just like a look at those files," Mark said. "What's the harm in that?"

Lou just shook his head, too frustrated to continue. so Freddy jumped in, flashing his smile.

"You've read my books, Mark," Freddy said, "so you know that this kind of thing happens all the time. Most serial killers never admit to all their kills. Ted Bundy, John Wayne Gacy and Robert Pickton are just a few well-known examples. It's common practice for law enforcement, if they can prove the case to *their* satisfaction, to close the files on murders they know a convicted serial killer committed, even if they can't prove it in court."

"I understand all that, Freddy. But I also know how eager homicide detectives are to clear cases. What could be more convenient than adding one more name to a serial killer's scorecard, just to get the file off your desk?"

Lou glared angrily at Mark. "Are you saying that's what happened here?"

"No, not at all," Mark replied. "And I mean no offense. After all, my son is a homicide detective, too. I'm just making a point. I'm not asking any of you to waste your time on this. I'd simply like to read the files on my own to satisfy my curiosity."

Tanis faced Lou and Freddy. "You might as well give it up. You don't know Mark Sloan as well as I do. It's futile arguing with him when he's curious about something. He never drops it. You will hear about this every day until he wears you down."

She looked at Mark and sighed, signaling her own surrender. "I'll get you the files, okay?"

"Great," Mark smiled. "Are we ready to move on?"

He slipped the Lydia Yates file under his seat for bedtime reading and reached into the box for another case.

Stanley Tidewell's surgeon stepped off the elevator into the Emergency Room. He'd been looking all over Community General Hospital for Dr. Travis, who hadn't responded to his pages. His search had brought him here, with a few frustrating detours. The surgeon had gotten lost in the maze of nearly identical corridors, which embarrassed him. He had no rational reason for being embarrassed. The hospital had changed a lot since the last time he'd been here. Actually, it had been rebuilt from the ground up, thanks to a bomber with a grudge against Mark Sloan.

As much as it had changed, it still felt like home to him, and he supposed it always would.

The surgeon approached a nurse at the front desk and showed her the visitor's pass that allowed him the privileges of a staff doctor. "I'm looking for Dr. Travis," he said politely. "Do you know where I can find him?"

"He's a little busy right now." She jerked her head towards the trauma room.

Curious, the surgeon went over for a peek.

Duke Gerbson, if he survived, could become a living argument for wearing seat belts. He wasn't wearing one when he veered to avoid a pipe on the freeway. His car slammed into a cement divider, but Duke kept going. Duke went through the windshield headfirst and tumbled down an embankment into a tangle of thorny bushes.

When the paramedics rolled him into the Community General Emergency Room he was unconscious, had difficulty breathing and had a bloody pulp where his face had once been, not to mention countless lacerations, large and small.

Now he was in the trauma room, with Dr. Jesse Travis and two nurses, Susan Hilliard and Teresa Chingas, trying to save his life.

While Jesse attempted to establish an airway, Susan and Teresa started an IV and attached electrodes to Duke's heavily tattooed chest to monitor his vital stats.

Jesse wanted to put a breathing tube in Duke's mouth and down his trachea. Problem was, Jesse had a hard time figuring out which gaping hole was Duke's mouth. And even if Jesse chose correctly, he wasn't sure he could find the trachea in all that gore.

"I'm gonna crike him," Jesse said, alerting the nurses that he was going to perform a cricothyrotomy. He took a scalpel and made a vertical cut directly into Duke's neck, just below his Adam's apple, exposing the cricothyroid membrane, then sliced into it to open the trachea.

Jesse made it look easy, but Susan knew the risks involved. He could just as easily have cut major nerves, veins or arteries, or damaged the esophagus, making an already deadly situation even worse. It took enormous skill and confidence to pull off the operation with such speed.

Susan handed him a breathing tube. Jesse inserted the tube into Duke's neck and it made a moist, sucking sound. It was just what they wanted to hear.

"We have a breather." Jesse stepped back, out of Susan's way.

Susan quickly hooked the tube up to a ventilator, trying to catch Jesse's eye to let him know how proud she was of him.

"His blood pressure is dropping, 60/40!" Teresa said urgently. "And I can't get a distal pulse."

Jesse quickly leaned forward with his

stethoscope, pressed it to Duke's chest and listened for breath sounds. The instant Jesse raised his head, someone pushed past him and stabbed a huge syringe into Duke's chest.

The intruder yanked the syringe out and tossed it on a tray. Duke's chest hissed like a punctured tire.

"He's breathing," Teresa said. "His blood pressure is rising."

"Classic tension pneumothorax," said Tidewell's surgeon, clearly pleased with himself.

Any doctor would have made the same diagnosis and done the same thing to relieve the pressure building up in Duke's chest. It was, in fact, exactly what Jesse was about to do when the stranger burst into the trauma room and did it for him. So it wasn't done to save the patient. It was done to humiliate Jesse. Which begged the question Jesse asked, shaking with rage.

"Who the hell do you think you are?"

"I'm pretty certain I'm Jack Stewart," the man said, climbing onto the table and straddling Duke's legs. "Would you mind holding his pelvis down? I'd like to save his leg."

Jesse did as he was told, too surprised by what he'd heard to put up a fight. *Jack*

71

Stewart? He was back? He glanced at Susan, who was staring right at him, bewildered. Jesse motioned to the patient. "Stabilize his neck."

Susan didn't try figuring out what was going on or why Jesse had given up control of the situation to a stranger; she just held Duke's neck firmly between her gloved hands. Teresa shifted her gaze between the monitors and Jack, her expression cold.

Jack grimaced and pulled Duke's hip joint back into place. Jesse felt the hip pop into position. Jack climbed off the table and dusted one hand off the other, indicating the end of a job well done. That was too much for Jesse. Whatever surprise he'd felt had worn off, replaced by anger.

Dr. Jack Stewart was Mark Sloan's old protégé. It took Jesse years to stop feeling like he was just this guy's replacement. And now Jack was back, undercutting him in front of everyone to prove what a hotshot he was. Word would be all over the hospital in fifteen minutes.

"How did you know his hip was dislocated?" Teresa asked.

Susan shot the nurse a furious look. By asking the question, Teresa was ceding even more authority to Jack than he'd already taken.

Teresa pretended not to notice and so did Jack, who happily answered the question. "First thing I saw when I walked in was that one of his legs was shorter than the other."

"Notice anything else?" she asked.

"Why? Did I miss something?"

Jesse gave the nurses some quick, pointed instructions, took Jack by the arm and led him into the hallway, out of earshot of Susan and Teresa, though he was certain they'd be watching.

Now that Jesse had a chance to really look at the guy, he reminded him of the kid who played Chachi on *Happy Days*, only twenty years older and twenty pounds heavier. Judging by the guy's rich, even tan, Jesse pegged Jack as one of those doctors who spent more time on the ski slopes than he did in the operating room. And Jesse noticed the Rolex, which was, after all, exactly why Jack wore the thing. Who needs a fifteen-thousand-dollar watch? Somebody who wants you to know they can afford a fifteen-thousand-dollar watch. Jesse hated him immediately and probably would have even without his big entrance.

"I don't care who you are —" Jesse began.

"Jack Stewart," Jack interrupted. "I thought we established that."

"Or why you're back —"

"I'm Stanley Tidewell's surgeon," Jack interrupted again. "You said you wanted to see me right away. So here I am."

Jack smiled amiably, which only made Jesse angrier.

"If you ever barge into my trauma room again, I will kick your ass so bad, you'll be the next patient."

"Not bad," Jack said. "But I'd work on that menacing squint you've got going. It looks like you've got something in your eye."

The smug, self-satisfied expression on Jack's face reminded Jesse that Jack reputedly came from a New York mob family. Jack had probably seen guys a lot tougher than him. Jesse wasn't going to intimidate him with talk. He had to show Jack he could back it up. Jesse tightened his fist and prepared to deck him.

But before Jesse could swing, Amanda Bentley pushed quickly past Jesse and nearly tackled Jack herself.

"Jack!" she squealed, giving him a big hug.

"Amanda." Jack lifted her off her feet and twirled her around. "Still as beautiful as ever."

She hadn't seen Jack in almost five years and though she told herself she'd never forgive him for the way he left, whatever lingering resentment she felt was overwhelmed, at least for the moment, by the joy of seeing him again.

"How long are you staying?" she asked.

"A couple days."

"Do Mark and Steve know you're back?"

"They do now," Jack said, looking over her shoulder.

Jesse turned just in time to see Mark rocketing up fast on his skate sneakers with a delighted smile on his face and way too much momentum behind him. There was no time for Jesse to escape, and Jesse knew it.

Mark stumbled trying to come to a running stop and plowed into Jesse. The impact knocked Jesse off his feet and sent him sliding on the floor, but Jack managed to catch Mark before he fell.

"Some things never change," Jack grinned, holding Mark up until he regained his balance.

"It's so good to see you, Jack," Mark said, overjoyed. "What brings you back to Community General?"

And why did you wait five years to do it, Mark thought, feeling the pain, and a little of the anger, all over again. The only contact he'd had with Jack, a man he once considered a surrogate son, was the occasional impersonal greeting card at Christmas or on his birthday.

"Stanley Tidewell asked me to fly in from Denver to do his kidney transplant," Jack said. "When he told me it was at Community General, I couldn't say no."

"Why didn't you tell us you were coming?" Amanda asked.

"I wanted it to be a surprise," Jack said.

"It certainly is," Mark said. "And a very welcome one, too. We have so much catching up to do!"

Nobody seemed to notice Jesse, who grabbed the railing on the wall for support and struggled to his feet. Mark, who was unfailingly polite, hadn't even bothered to apologize for knocking him down. It was as if Jesse was invisible. And Jesse knew that's how he would remain as long as Jack Stewart was around.

Jesse turned and saw Susan watching him through the trauma room window. She'd seen it all and from the look on her face understood what it meant, too.

The day had started out bad and just kept getting worse, heaping humiliation on top of humiliation. Jesse was about to walk quietly away when Mark called out to him.

"Hey, Jesse," Mark said. "Have you met Jack yet?"

CHAPTER FIVE

Mark invited everyone to the beach house for dinner and he insisted that Jesse and Susan come as well. He said he wanted the whole family together.

The comment made Jesse feel better and for a while made him think he'd judged Mark too harshly earlier at the hospital. But a few minutes after arriving, Jesse quickly reversed his opinion again. Mark, Steve, Amanda and Jack immediately started reminiscing about their past adventures together, in the good old days before Jack left and his replacement arrived.

Jack recalled fondly the time Mark talked him into going undercover as a Los Angeles County lifeguard to help expose a killer on the beach.

Mark remembered when he'd been framed for the murder of his accountant, and Jack smuggled him out of the hospital, past a phalanx of police officers, by putting him in a body bag.

Amanda talked about the time her business manager stole all her money, spent it on paintings and disappeared. "I was literally living in the doctor's lounge, completely broke, and Jack saved me," she said, laughing about it now.

She described how Jack pretended to be an art thief and brought the fugitive money manager out of hiding by offering to sell him stolen masterpieces. Amanda ended up getting all of her money back.

"Thanks to you, Amanda, I almost got arrested by the FBI," Jack said. "And I got thrown out the window of a high-rise hotel."

"Good thing the room had a view of the swimming pool," Steve said, then regaled everyone with the story of how he and Jack, at Mark's urging, infiltrated a dating service to flush out a "psycho babe" who was killing single men.

"Somehow Jack ended up with all the airline stewardesses, lifeguards and aspiring actresses," Steve said. "I got the ones with uncontrollable flatulence, Tourette's Syndrome, narcolepsy and, best of all, the woman who wanted to cut me into bite-size pieces with her huge butcher knife."

"It was the best thing that ever happened to your love life," Jack said. "You finally had one."

Jesse laughed along with the rest of them, just to be polite, but he found nothing funny about it. He hid his discomfort well, because Mark certainly didn't seem to notice it.

For Mark, it was the perfect evening. A warm night by the beach, good food and a house full of close friends rejoicing in each other's company.

"So, what's it been like living in Denver?" Mark asked cheerfully.

"Oddly enough, I've managed to practice medicine for five years without investigating a single homicide," Jack said. "You had me believing being a detective was part of the job."

"It isn't?" Jesse asked, venturing his first contribution to the conversation besides a fake guffaw or two. He was rewarded with genuine laughter all around and an appreciative smile from Susan.

"I see you've conned another resident, Mark," Jack said.

"All good doctors have to be good detectives, too," Mark explained innocently. "You have to analyze the clues the body gives you to make an accurate diagnosis. I was simply trying to help you both hone that essential skill by applying it to other problems."

Mark remembered what Jack Stewart had been like when he first met him. Quiet, brooding, the first member of his mob family to become a doctor, to completely turn his back on the "business" he was expected to join. Jack changed his last name and fled as far west as he could go from his family and still remain in the continental United States. Even so, Jack was self-conscious, certain his family's reputation was something he wore like skin.

Perhaps that was why Jack was so eager to help Mark in his crime-solving pursuits, to somehow prove to himself, and to the world, just how different he was from the family he came from.

And now look at him, Mark thought. *A successful, respected surgeon in his own right.* Jack was now a man secure in the knowledge that he was judged solely on the strength of his own character and not his family's.

Amanda raised her hand to get everyone's attention. "I'd just like to point out, for the record, that I'm the only doctor here with an honest excuse to poke around homicides. Face it, you all want to be me."

"I just want your money," Jack said.

"Oh, give me a break," Steve said. "I saw that Rolex on your wrist. You're loaded.

How many days a week do you actually work?"

Jack grinned. "Three."

"And you aren't using all that free time to solve crimes?" Steve said. "What kind of doctor are you?"

One who, they learned, operated a high-end practice out of a renovated Victorian mansion. One who regularly spoke at scholarly conferences and had been published in all the top journals in his field. One who owned a ski lodge in Aspen and a new Mercedes SL and went on sportfishing expeditions with other rich, handsome surgeons to Russia, Alaska and South America. One who made Jesse sick and Mark enormously proud.

"No wonder you ran away," Amanda said pointedly.

It was as if she'd just pointed to the big zit on someone's nose that everyone else had politely pretended not to notice.

There was an uncomfortable silence. Uncomfortable for everyone but Jesse, who was glad to see Jack squirm for the first time since he'd made his surprise reappearance.

That's when the doorbell rang. Steve hopped up to get it, and Mark used the interruption as an excuse to change the subject by asking everyone if they needed refills on their drinks.

Mark was handing out more soft drinks when Tanis Archer came in, toting a big cardboard box.

"Sorry to intrude on your party," Tanis said to Mark. "But I got the files you asked for."

Mark introduced Tanis to Jack, the only person in the room she didn't already know, then briefly explained that the files related to his work on the chief's Blue Ribbon Task Force on Unsolved Homicides.

Jack tipped his head towards the box. "I'd be glad to look over the files with you and offer my expert opinion."

Expert opinion? Who was this guy kidding? Jesse thought. It was more than Jesse could stand. The remark might have been more tolerable if Jesse hadn't forgotten that he'd made Mark the same offer himself, in almost the same words, just a few days ago.

Jesse motioned to Susan that it was time to go. She started to gather her things together.

"I appreciate the offer, Jack," Mark said. "But as much as I'd like your input, I'm afraid the work of the task force has to remain confidential."

"If you change your mind, Mark, you know I'm here if you need me."

You used to be, Mark thought. Once again he wondered, as he had many times before, what made Jack leave so quickly and then keep his distance from them for so long.

Mark noticed Jesse and Susan getting up to leave. "Going so soon?"

"Susan has an early shift tomorrow," Jesse said. It was news to Susan, but she quickly nodded her head in agreement. Jesse waved at the group. "Good night, everyone."

"Wait a second, Jesse," Mark said, then turned to Jack. "There is one thing you can do for me, Jack. Because of my task force obligations, I won't be able to participate in Stanley's transplant operation. I'd appreciate it if you'd let Jesse take my place." Mark faced Jesse. "If you don't mind, of course."

Jack and Jesse both contrived smiles for Mark's benefit.

"Sure," Jack said.

"No problem," Jesse said, putting his hand on Susan's back and gently nudging her towards the front door.

"It's been a lovely evening, Dr. Sloan," Susan said.

"You're welcome any time, Susan," he

said with a smile. "And please, it's Mark to my friends."

She couldn't bring herself to call him Mark, even though he'd asked her to many times. Dr. Sloan offered her that courtesy, that familiarity, because he knew how Jesse felt about her, not because Dr. Sloan liked her, or felt close to her or truly respected her in any way. Calling him Mark would have implied a friendship she didn't feel yet and, she was certain, neither did he.

Jesse hustled her out the door as quickly as he could without appearing rude to his hosts. But Mark wasn't as insensitive to what Jesse was feeling as the young doctor thought. It was natural that Jesse would feel threatened by Jack, and more than a little competitive towards him. It was one reason Mark insisted on Jesse taking part in Stanley's operation, to force them to learn to work together and to recognize each other's talents. Even so, Mark made a mental note to show Jesse a little extra attention and to remind him just how good a doctor he was. And, he thought, it wouldn't hurt to find a moment to let Susan know how much respect she'd earned among the doctors and the nursing staff at Community General.

Mark turned back to his guests as Tanis

settled into the leather armchair, a mug of hot coffee in her hands. She looked very comfortable. Ordinarily, that wouldn't have bothered him. She would have been welcome. He glanced at Jack and Amanda, sharing a laugh. They didn't seem to be in any hurry to go, either. And there was Steve coming out of the kitchen with a fresh bowl of chips and dip, one more incentive for them to stay. It could be another couple of hours before they were gone now, Mark thought, feeling a stab of guilt.

The truth was, he wished they'd all followed Jesse out the door. Ever since Tanis walked in with the box, all he wanted to do was abandon the party and start reading the files it contained.

Maybe he could.

He glanced at the box of files and felt an almost magnetic pull towards it. He looked around the room. No one was paying any attention to him. He wouldn't be missed for a while.

"Did you hear that guy blather on and on about what a great doctor he is? About the marlin he caught off Cabo? About the special paint job on his Mercedes?" Jesse steered his Mustang convertible away from

Mark's house and merged into the light traffic on Pacific Coast Highway. "I'm surprised he didn't whip out his bank statements and pass them around the room."

"He's a pig," Susan said, her voice dripping with disgust.

Jesse expected Susan to be supportive, but the intensity of her dislike surprised him. What could Jack have done to make her so upset? Then it hit him. He changed lanes so he'd be ready to make a sudden U-turn and go back to the beach house if he had to.

"He'd didn't make a pass at you, did he?"

"No, nothing like that. You know Teresa Chingas?"

Jesse nodded. She was the nurse who had worked with them in the trauma room on the guy who'd lost his face.

"After Jack left the ER, she just fell apart," Susan said. "She couldn't stop crying for about twenty minutes."

"I didn't know she cared that much about me."

Susan looked at him in disbelief. "She wasn't crying about you. It was about him."

Now Jesse was thoroughly confused. "Why?"

"Because Jack said the first thing he noticed when he came in was that patient's leg. And when Teresa asked him if he noticed anything else, he said no."

"So?"

"So he didn't notice *her*."

"She's pretty, but not enough to distract a doctor from a guy dying on the table." Even as he said it, he couldn't believe he was now defending a man that two seconds ago he was trashing. "Why's she so full of herself?"

"This from the guy who thought she was crying over him."

"Then what was it?"

"Teresa and Jack were dating before he left L.A. It was pretty serious. Now he doesn't even recognize her. How can you be that close to someone and then completely forget them?"

"Maybe he wasn't as close to her as she thought he was."

"*Duh*, you think?" She shook her head angrily and turned her attention to the Santa Monica Pier, the lights of the Ferris wheel reflecting off the inky surf.

Jesse kept quiet, afraid to say anything that might make things worse, and tried to figure out how the conversation had turned against him. Whatever the answer was, it was Jack Stewart's fault.

There was a postcard available for every San Francisco landmark Jean-Marc Gaddois photographed with his disposable camera during his vacation. The postcards had better pictures taken by professional photographers with great cameras. Once you factored in the cost of film and developing, the postcards were a lot cheaper than what he was spending on his badly composed, uninspired and technically flawed pictures.

That kind of stupidity was reason enough to kill the French tourist, not that the killer needed another one. There was no shortage of reasons why Jean-Marc Gaddois had to die. There were two, though, that especially bugged the Killer. The incomprehensible, heavily accented English that Jean-Marc inflicted on humanity when he opened his big, croissant-munching maw to ask for directions to places that were clearly indicated on the Michelin guide map in his back pocket. And the disgusting, hand-rolled cigarettes that he constantly smoked, filling streets, restaurants and hotels with the stench of blazing Parisian dung. The list was endless and painfully obvious and would grow every day until Jean-Marc Gaddois was mercifully put down.

The Killer had nothing against the French,

per se. Nothing he didn't also hold against the Japanese, the Germans, the Iranians, the Dutch, the Italians, the Norwegians, the Russians, the Spanish and the hordes of other foreigners invading our soil. And that included Canadians, who didn't fool him one bit.

It was a cool, windy, noisy night in the City. The smell of seagulls and fish and salt water spread from the Bay across the entire city. The scrappy little Frenchman, trying to fit in with his Ray-Bans and his pleated Ralph Lauren shorts and polo shirt, his disposable camera in his disposable hand, rode up the escalator from the underground Powell Street BART station.

He emerged on the street and immediately took a flash picture of the subway escalator he just stepped off, blinding the bystander behind him, then began the uphill trek to his hotel near Union Square.

Jean-Marc passed an alley and heard someone beckon to him in French.

Excusez-moi, je suis perdu, the Killer said. Pouvez vous m'indiquer oò est Fisherman's Wharf?

Oui, naturellement, mon ami, Jean-Marc whipped out his handy Michelin guide and stepped into the alley. He might have asked himself, if he'd had another thirty seconds to live, why a fellow stinking Frenchman was standing in a garbage-strewn alley waiting for another stinking Frenchman to wander by with a map.

The Killer pulled a gun from his jacket, jammed a raw potato on the end of the barrel and shot Jean-Marc point-blank in the chest. The potato exploded but muffled most of the distinctive sound of the gunshot. Anyone hearing it would have mistaken it for a firecracker.

Jean-Marc fell flat on his back, stone dead and wide-eyed in shock, flecks of raw potato in his hair.

The Killer pried Jean-Marc's disposable camera from his hand and took a picture, capturing a view of San Francisco that certainly wouldn't be found on any postcard.

CHAPTER SIX

Steve got up at six in the morning and did his regular two-mile run up the beach, checking out the houses as he ran, partly out of cop habit and partly to catch a glimpse of any celebrities who might be out exercising early.

It was a pricey, and exclusive, stretch of sand. Most of the houses on Broad Beach belonged to actors, directors, big-shot producers and a few overcompensated, perk-fat CEOs. Mark got in on a fluke. He'd bought the house from the Drug Enforcement Agency, who'd seized it with all the other assets belonging to a Columbian druglord they'd arrested. A DEA buddy tipped Mark off about the house. Mark made an offer on the property before it could be auctioned off to the public. It was a steal, albeit a legal one. Mark was always lucky that way.

That morning, Steve didn't spot any Oscar winners out on the sand, so he thought about the previous night and his mixed feelings about seeing Jack Stewart again. He genuinely liked Jack but couldn't help feeling resentful towards him. It wasn't Jack's fault; it was Mark's. Steve didn't understand his father's need to keep grooming doctors in his own image. It wouldn't bother Steve if Mark was just guiding them through the world of medicine. It was when Mark started training them as detectives that Steve felt uncomfortable.

He knew his father was proud of his work as a homicide detective, but he couldn't help feeling that Mark was disappointed in him for not pursuing medicine, too, and that befriending first Jack, and then Jesse, was proof of that.

Steve never asked Mark directly about it; he sort of asked questions around the issue, a technique Mark had actually taught him. Mark seemed to think Jack and Jesse showed a genuine interest in detective work. Besides, Mark had another excuse. He often needed some legwork done on his investigations, and he couldn't ask Steve to do it, not without putting Steve's job in jeopardy.

That much was true. Still, Steve never quite accepted the explanation. He sometimes asked himself if he'd gone into the restaurant business with Jesse just to shoe-horn himself into the young doctor's relationship with Mark.

That kind of thinking only made Steve angry with himself, made him feel petty and childish, so he put it out of his head as quickly as he could.

It helped that he was distracted by a certain Oscar-nominated actress jogging by, taking her new breast implants out for some air. He ran an extra mile just to enjoy the view.

When Steve got back to the house, he went upstairs and was surprised to see Mark at the kitchen table, still in his clothes from last night, surrounded by the files Tanis had brought over and one of Freddy Meeks' true crime books. Steve grabbed a Gatorade from the refrigerator and joined Mark at the table.

"You stayed up all night looking at the files?" Steve asked.

Mark took off his glasses and rubbed his bloodshot eyes. "I couldn't help myself."

"I didn't realize the task force was on a deadline."

"We aren't," Mark said. "And these aren't even unsolved homicides that I'm looking at."

"Then what are you doing?"

"I'm not exactly sure," Mark said. "It started out as curiosity and now that I've read the files, something is troubling me."

Uh-oh. Steve knew what that usually meant. Hours of extra work in addition to his regular case load, chasing down leads for his father. The upside was, those leads usually panned out and led to the conviction of a murderer.

"What's troubling you?" Steve asked.

"I can't pin it down," Mark replied. "It's just a feeling."

That was usually worse than if Mark actually had a lead to go on. It meant twice as many extra hours of work for Steve gathering information to help his dad shape the feeling into something substantial they could work with. But there was no way around it. This was part of Mark Sloan's process.

"Well, tell me what you've got," Steve said. "Maybe whatever it is will become clear to you when you go through all the facts again."

It was a long shot, Steve thought, but he knew how his father absorbed information. He never discounted a fact, no matter how insignificant. Any normal person would get lost in the sheer quantity and have to filter some of it out in order to focus their thoughts. But for Mark, it was the opposite. There were never too many details he was willing to consider. What might seem pointless or insignificant at first could later become the most vital clue in the case. Forcing his dad to explain the situation to him, to bring order to the chaos of facts swirling in his head, might help Mark bring what was troubling him into focus.

Mark referred to a legal pad full of notes. "The Reaper killed nine women. He was prosecuted, and convicted, for six of them. The other three victims are attributed to him because the details of their killings were consistent with the other murders. Those details were closely guarded and never released to the media until the Reaper went on trial, so copycat killings were ruled out."

Mark explained to Steve the similarities between the three victims — Sarah Clarke, Emilia Santiago and Lydia Yates — and the six other victims. They were all single women, slightly on the dowdy side. They all worked secretarial or temp clerical jobs. They all were out running errands when they were killed. Sarah was at the mall. Emilia was buying batteries at Sav-on. Lydia was doing her grocery shopping. They were all attacked from behind, their necks broken. They were all driven in their own cars by the killer to where their bodies were dumped; then their cars were returned to the parking lots where he'd found them. Sarah's body was left at the beach. Emilia was found in an abandoned warehouse. Lydia was stuffed in a sewer pipe. The murders also occurred in the same geographical area as the other six killings and fell within the Reaper's rough pattern of one new victim every two weeks.

"What about physical evidence?" Steve asked.

"There wasn't any," Mark said, laying out photos of the crime scenes. "All they recovered was the trash where the victims were dumped. Cigarette butts, bottle caps, gum wrappers, the usual. All of it was tested for prints and DNA, of course. None of it was ever matched to the Reaper. But once they caught him in their sting, they were able to backtrack his movements and get enough evidence to tie him to six of the killings."

Steve sorted through the pictures, stacked them neatly and passed them back to Mark. "The prosecutors picked the cases that they thought were the strongest, the ones they knew they could win convictions on, and pursued those. That doesn't mean the other cases weren't good, just not *as* good."

"I know," Mark said.

"So what's the problem?"

"I don't know."

"But you never ignore that feeling, do you?"

"I'd love to; it just won't let me," Mark said. "It will keep me up nights, nag at me all day and never give me any peace until I give in."

"Funny, that's how a lot of people describe you."

"Then no one can accuse me of treating them differently than I treat myself," Mark said with a smile.

"I'm sure that will give them a lot of comfort." Steve finished his bottle of Gatorade and glanced at his watch. He had about thirty minutes to shower and get to work. He was going to be late. "What's your next move?"

Mark picked up *Reaper Madness*, Freddy's book, and glanced at the cover, a lurid picture of a woman in a parking lot, her back to the ominous shadow approaching her.

"I guess there's only one thing I can do," Mark said. "Face the Reaper."

Billy Tidewell was in his hospital gown, sitting on top of his bed and watching a college football game when Jesse came in to tell him the details of the operation he'd be having in just a few hours.

But Billy seemed more interested in following the game than in learning how Jesse would be removing his kidney and how Jack, moments later, would be implanting it in his father.

Either Billy had remarkable faith in his doctors or he kept his fear in check by avoiding the details — or he simply didn't care.

Jesse told him the nurse would be coming in to take his pre-op blood test and then they'd be ready to go. Billy had just one question.

"Think somebody could tape the game for me?" Billy asked.

Jesse said he'd see if he could find a blank tape and record it for him on the VCR in the doctor's lounge.

On the way out of the room, Jesse ran into Jack. They faced each other awkwardly.

"I was just coming in to brief the patient," Jack said.

"I already have," Jesse said. "He's more

98

interested in the UCLA game."

"I don't blame him," Jack said. "I've got some serious money riding on it. Think somebody could tape it for me?"

"Sure."

Jesse started to go, but Jack stopped him. "Look, I want to apologize for what happened in the E.R. I wasn't trying to show off or anything. I was looking for you, I saw that guy's problem and I jumped in without thinking. I would have done the same thing if it was Mark standing there instead of you."

Which says volumes about you, Jesse thought. "It's okay; no problem."

"Then shake my hand."

"What?"

"Shake my hand," Jack stuck out his hand to Jesse. "We're starting over. I'm Jack Stewart. I'm pleased you'll be assisting me in this operation."

"Yeah, whatever." Jesse shook his hand and walked away. Jack wasn't going to get off that easy for his arrogance. Maybe that slick charm worked on other people, but not Jesse Travis.

Jack shrugged it off and went into Billy's room to introduce himself and catch a few minutes of the game. When Susan came in to take Billy's blood, Jack took that as his cue to leave. He told Billy he'd see him in the recovery room after the operation, and if he didn't mind some company, maybe they'd catch the end of the game together on tape.

Jack left, caught an empty elevator and started to review Stanley's file again as he rode down to the second floor. He didn't notice when the elevator stopped on the fourth floor and someone else came in. He didn't notice the other passenger until the elevator came to a jarring stop between floors.

He looked up and saw the other passenger was Amanda, and from the hard expression on her face, she meant business.

"Why did you stop the elevator?" Jack asked.

"Why did you leave?" Amanda asked, her firm voice making it less a question than a demand.

"C'mon, Amanda, I'm heading into the O.R. Can't this wait?"

"It has, for five years. I want to know why you didn't tell us about the job offer in Denver until the day you were leaving."

"You know I don't like good-byes. All those tears and hugs and things. It was better that way."

"Not good enough." Amanda crossed

her arms beneath her chest. "It doesn't explain why you left. It doesn't explain why we've barely heard from you since then."

"I don't want to get into this now."

"Or ever. That's why I'm holding you prisoner in this elevator until I get answers."

Jack knew Amanda was serious. He'd seen that look of stony determination, and that don't-mess-with-me posture, many times before. If he made a move for the elevator controls, he had no doubt she'd knee him in the groin or break his wrist.

"They were offering me big money, certainly a lot more than I was making here," Jack said. "I wanted it; I wanted it bad."

"What's wrong with that?"

"I was afraid all of you would think I was selling out," Jack replied. "That I was throwing away the special thing we all had going just for a paycheck."

"Nobody would have thought that," Amanda said. "We would have been happy for you."

"C'mon, Amanda," Jack said. "If we weren't in the hospital, we were on the street, helping Mark with his cases. We weren't supposed to be thinking about money. We were supposed to be thinking only about helping patients and solving murders. If I told you that I'd got the offer, and that I was seriously considering it, you never would have looked at me the same way again. None of you would."

"That's not true," Amanda said.

"You know Mark was grooming me to be just like him," Jack said. "What would he have said if I told him I cared more about making money than being Mark Sloan Jr. I didn't want to hurt him."

"Running away was a much better idea." Amanda hit the stop button again, and the elevator started moving again, arriving almost immediately at the next floor. "I'm sure that didn't hurt at all. Good thinking, Jack."

The elevator doors opened and Amanda marched out, leaving Jack behind, watching her.

The name Sunrise Valley typically conjured up visions of a lush, green paradise of sparkling rivers, abundant fruit and plentiful game. It was one thing to slap the name on a golf course, a condo community, a retirement home or even a trailer park. Giving the name to a high-security prison for extremely violent offenders seemed like a cruel joke.

Sunrise Valley State Prison was 170

miles north of Los Angeles, built amidst endless cotton fields and on a dry lake that had once been home to Pleistocene mammals and the Tachi Yokut tribe of Indians.

Now it was home to over five thousand murderers and rapists in facilities meant to hold half that many. The deadliest killers were kept in the Secure Housing Unit, a high-security facility separate from the general prison population. The overcrowding forced Black and Latino rival gangs to share the same cramped space, not only with each other, but with the Aryan Brotherhood and the Klan. The inevitable bloody clashes weren't accidental. Correction officials intentionally pitted gangs against gangs to brutalize each other into what they termed "a more manageable and cooperative inmate population."

The guards were known for being every bit as sadistic as their prisoners. Several correctional officers were prosecuted for staging gladiator battles among the most hardened offenders and betting on the deadly outcome.

So it was no wonder that Mark walked into Sunrise Valley State Prison with trepidation. It was not a place he looked forward to visiting. But it was the only place he'd find the answer to one simple question: *Did the Reaper kill Sarah Clarke, Emilia Santiago and Lydia Yates?* Neal Winnick, also known as the Reaper, had nothing to lose by answering it. And if he answered it quickly enough, Mark could be out of there in five minutes.

Mark had little hope that things would go that smoothly. Killers like Winnick got off toying with people, and this encounter would be no exception. Mark had seen the courtroom photos of Winnick, his eyes radiating cold, calculated evil, and he'd read the interviews with the killer in Freddy's book. Winnick was a cunning, egotistical killer who relished fear and manipulation. The serial killer would exercise his obsessions on Mark Sloan, if for no other reason than to entertain himself, to break the crushing monotony of prison life.

Mark waited in the interview room. He noticed the steel table and two chairs were bolted to the floor. There was a ring imbedded in the concrete in front of each chair to secure the chains that bound the prisoners. Before entering the room, Mark was searched for anything that Winnick could conceivably use as a weapon or a tool. Mark emptied his pockets, handing over his belt, tie, wallet, keys, watch and pen, as well as the laces from his shoes and his reading glasses. His sport jacket was taken, too, leaving Mark in just his shirt-sleeves and slacks.

All the precautions didn't make Mark feel any safer. They made him even more nervous. They painted a picture of a super-human creature of evil, able to turn a strand of hair into a dagger or morph like the Incredible Hulk into a raging, homicidal monster.

What was he doing here? Did he really want to be alone with someone this unbelievably dangerous?

Mark heard the clank of the door lock sliding open. It was too late to leave now. The heavy steel door opened and two guards led Neal Winnick into the room. Winnick shuffled to the table and stood shivering in his sweat-soaked, orange jumpsuit while a guard attached his leg and ankle chains to the ring on the floor.

Mark used the moment to study Winnick. It was hard to believe this was the same man Mark saw in the courtroom photos. His skin was ghostly pale. His eyes, which had once radiated such evil, were vacant. He was gaunt and clearly terrified. He'd been broken. The guards left and Winnick sat across from Mark, refusing to meet his eyes.

"I'm Dr. Mark Sloan. I've been appointed to a task force investigating unsolved murders."

Winnick hugged himself and tried to control his shaking. "You have to get me out of here."

"You killed nine women; you're never getting out," Mark said. "It was nine women, right? They wouldn't let me bring in my notes. I guess they were afraid you might use the paper to kill me."

Winnick started to sob. "Please, I can't go back in."

Mark studied Winnick for any signs of physical abuse but couldn't see anything. But something had clearly been done to him. Something awful.

"Go back where?" Mark asked.

"I'm suffocating," Winnick screeched. "Take me outside! Tell them I have to go outside!"

Mark could see he wouldn't get any answers out of Winnick and whatever he did get couldn't be trusted. This man was insane. He got up and pressed the buzzer on the wall. The guards came back, unlocked Winnick and lifted him from his seat. Winnick had wet himself.

"Don't take me back!" Winnick yelled. "No!"

A jowly-faced guard stayed behind with Mark as the sniveling murderer was led away.

"They used to call him the Reaper, can you believe it?" the guard said. "Look at him now, pissing his own pants."

"What did you do to him?" Mark asked.

"Nobody had to do nothing to him except lock him in his little cell," the guard said, then added with a grin, "The littler, the better."

Suddenly, Mark understood what was happening. Winnick's captivity was driving him insane, the endless days of unrelenting terror slowly eroding his mind.

The Reaper was claustrophobic.

CHAPTER SEVEN

The surgery to remove Billy Tidewell's kidney only took about an hour. Jesse opened up Billy's belly, moved his intestines aside to allow access to the kidney and then clamped off the renal artery and vein. He cut the ureter and removed the kidney, which he placed in a blue plastic pan. The scrub nurse, Teresa Chingas, poured saline over the organ and carried the pan to an adjoining operating room, where Jack Stewart was waiting, his patient Stanley Tidewell slit open and ready for implantation.

Jesse took another half hour to finish up, close his incision and send Billy into recovery. Then he changed into new scrubs, washed his hands again and went into the adjoining operating room to watch Jack complete the transplant.

Jack removed Stanley's failed kidney and implanted Billy's healthy one in its place, reattaching the renal artery and veins to the new organ. He attached the ureter to the bladder with a small plastic catheter.

Jesse had to admire the surgeon's expert handiwork. Jack was a jerk, Jesse thought, but he was definitely an artist in the operating room.

Approximately three hours after the operation began, Jack sewed Stanley's abdomen closed and was ready to send his patient to the Intensive Care Unit for twenty-four hours of careful observation. For the first day, Jesse knew, it was going to be necessary to monitor the organ closely and suppress Stanley's immune system with a battery of antirejection drugs.

Jack looked up, spotted Jesse standing in the corner and gave him the thumbs-up.

Jesse flashed the same signal in return. There was no doubt about Jack's prowess in the operating room. And he had to give the guy credit for apologizing, even if he was a little too smooth about it. Perhaps, Jesse thought, he ought to give Jack a second chance.

Suddenly the anesthesiologist shouted, "His blood pressure is dropping!"

Almost immediately, Stanley started wheezing. Jack and Jesse shared a look. *Bronchospasm!*

Jack immediately started giving orders to the nurses. "One half cc. of epinephrine,

109

push sixteen milligrams of decadron, a hundred milligrams of benedryl IV and start a dopamine drip!"

The nurses did as they were told, pumping the drugs into his veins, but Stanley's blood pressure continued to plummet. He was going into pulmonary edema. Jack worked frantically to save his patient. Jesse didn't move from the corner. He knew there was nothing he could do that Jack wasn't already doing. Jesse also knew what would happen next.

The EKG emitted its high-pitched alarm.

Stanley was going into cardiac arrest.

"The Reaper didn't kill Lydia Yates," Mark Sloan said, surveying his skeptical audience.

Lou Rozan, Freddy Meeks and Tanis Archer were there of course, and so was Police Chief Masters, looking especially uncomfortable in the tiny basement room he'd selected as the headquarters for the task force. Masters could just as easily have invited them all up to his spacious office, with its expansive views of downtown Los Angeles, but it would have undercut his subtle message. The task force had its place, and it was in the deepest, darkest corner of the LAPD. To bring them up for even a moment into the daylight, into the echelons of power, would have lent more credibility and visibility to the task force than Masters wanted to give it. So here Masters was, reluctantly responding to Mark's urgent phone call.

"As I recall, Dr. Sloan, I specifically stated that the mandate of this task force was to reexamine inactive homicide cases, not to reopen successful prosecutions," Masters said.

"This case was never actually prosecuted," Mark said. "And for good reason. The killer hasn't been caught yet."

Mark pointed to a poster board he'd made, which he'd propped up on boxes so everyone could see it. The board showed pictures of each of the Reaper's nine victims, with details of their homicides listed as bullet points beneath them.

"Notice where the bodies were dumped. The beach. A vacant lot. An abandoned warehouse. A playground. All the bodies were left in large or open spaces, except one. Lydia Yates." Mark tapped her picture with his finger. "She was stuffed into a sewer pipe."

"So? I don't see the significance," Lou said.

"Neal Winnick is claustrophobic," Mark said. "That's why all the bodies were found in large or open spaces. He never would have crawled into that pipe."

"How do you know he's claustrophobic?" Freddy asked. "I certainly didn't notice it."

"I know; I read your book," Mark said. "My guess is that Winnick was able to control his terror, or at least hide it, during the trial. But he can't anymore. I visited him. I saw what imprisonment is doing to him."

"There are a lot of reasons for a guy to go wacko in prison," Tanis said. "That doesn't mean he's afraid of being in closed spaces."

"I thought about that, too," said Mark. "Then I reread the case file. His mother used to lock him in the closet for days at a time. As an adult, Winnick lived in a large, converted warehouse and worked as a park ranger, a job that kept him outdoors."

"It makes sense," Lou Rozan said softly. "And it does fit in with his hatred, and fear, of women."

"That's it?" Chief Masters sighed. "That's all you have?"

"There's more," Mark said. "The Reaper used the victims' cars to dispose of the bodies. He had to adjust the drivers' seats. In every car but one, the seat was twenty inches from the gas pedal, suggesting the killer was about five foot eleven. It was a significant enough fact to make it into Lou's profile of the killer which, as we all know, turned out to be amazingly accurate. But the driver's seat in Lydia Yates' car was seventeen inches from the gas pedal. Whoever killed her was about five foot eight."

Mark stopped for a moment to let the facts sink in; then he looked directly at the chief. "Whoever killed Lydia Yates wanted it to look like the Reaper did it. And whoever killed her is still out there."

The chief cleared his throat and flicked away some imaginary lint from his sleeve. "Based on the adjustment of a car seat and your *assumption* that Winnick is claustrophobic, you expect me to reopen the investigation into Lydia Yates' murder."

"That's right," Mark replied.

The chief glanced at the other task force members, particularly Tanis Archer. "Do you all agree?"

"I think it's worth considering," Tanis replied.

"Not if it means I have to rewrite my book," Freddy said with a smile, attempting to add some levity. He failed, at least with the chief.

"It would mean a lot more than that, Mr. Meeks," Masters snapped. "It would mean reopening the entire Reaper investigation and jeopardizing his conviction."

"But Winnick wasn't convicted of her murder, it was just assumed —" Mark began, but the chief interrupted him.

"I'm not talking about the law here, Dr. Sloan. I'm talking about political realities. If we were to suggest we were wrong about him being responsible for *this* murder, it would cast doubt on *all* the murders he committed. The media, the ACLU and every civil rights group in the country would start crawling all over the Reaper investigation. The speculation could even spread to other serial-killer cases we've prosecuted."

"Now that you mention it, I —" Mark began, but the chief cut him off again.

"Have you thought about the Yates family, Dr. Sloan? Have you considered how emotionally devastating this irresponsible speculation of yours would be to them?"

"I think they'd want their daughter's killer punished for what he did."

"They got that," the chief said emphatically, rising from his seat and towering over Mark. "The man who killed their daughter is in prison. The case is closed. I suggest you put your considerable energy into investigating cases that aren't solved, rather than trying to undo the ones that are."

The chief glared at Mark with contempt, then turned to face the others.

"In the future, you are to restrict your inquiries to the files *in this room*," Masters said pointedly, then drilled Tanis Archer with his gaze. "Is that clear?"

"Yes, sir," Tanis said.

Masters marched out, ducking a bit to clear the doorway. Lou picked up his box lunch and rose from his seat.

"I think that's enough for today," Lou said. "Interesting theory, Dr. Sloan, but I have to agree with the chief. It's pretty thin. I'm still convinced the right man is on death row."

Freddy got up, too. "I'm just glad I don't have to call my publisher and tell him I got it wrong. Wouldn't do much for sales of my next book. Nice presentation, though. Loved the poster boards."

The two men left. After a moment, Mark turned to Tanis. "I hope I didn't get you in too much trouble."

Tanis shook her head. "I can't be worse off than I already am."

"I'm relieved to hear you say that," Mark

said, "because I'll need the files on every serial-killer investigation in the last ten years, specifically those in which there were murders attributed to the killer that he wasn't prosecuted for."

"Those files aren't in this room," Tanis said.

"Not yet," Mark smiled. "But they will be as soon as you bring them."

That's when Mark's pager went off. When he saw the number, he knew something horrible had happened.

The page was from the hospital morgue.

CHAPTER EIGHT

The pathology lab at Community General Hospital doubled as the Adjunct County Medical Examiner's office and morgue. Both were the domain of Dr. Amanda Bentley, who stood at the head of a stainless-steel table in the center of the room. Laid out in front of her was Stanley Tidewell's corpse. Mark and Jesse stood on one side of the table, Jack on the other. They all were staring down at the body, which was quickly becoming as cold as the room.

"I don't understand how this could have happened," Mark said.

"You and me both," Jack said.

"It looks like he died from a massive heart attack," Amanda said, "but I won't be able to isolate the exact cause of death until I complete my autopsy."

"The operation went through without a hitch," Jack said. "There were no signs that anything was wrong."

"There are now," Mark said, then looked at Jesse. "Do you have anything to add?"

"Everything looked okay to me, too." Jesse could see that Jack was relieved. "Both Stanley and Billy were checked thoroughly for compatibility before the operation. And the pre-op blood work was completely clean."

"You're all trying to reach a conclusion without the benefit of the facts," Amanda said. "Give me the night. I'll have something for you to go on in the morning."

That was her not-so-subtle way of throwing them out and they knew it. The three men shuffled away, leaving Amanda alone to complete her grim task.

In the corridor, Mark pulled Jack and Jesse aside. "Has anyone told Stanley's son yet?"

Jesse shook his head. "He's still in recovery. He should be waking up soon."

Jack took a deep breath. "I'll tell him."

"I don't think that would be a good idea," Mark said. "I've known the family a long time. I should do it."

"But it's not your fault," Jack said.

"We don't know that it's anybody's fault," Mark replied. "Both of you go home and get some rest."

Jack headed for the elevator and a long, lonely, soul-searching night at his hotel.

Jesse took the stairs up to the doctors'

lounge, where his girlfriend Susan was waiting for him to take her home.

And Mark Sloan closed his eyes for a moment, summoned his strength and walked towards the recovery room to do something he had unfortunately done many times before. He would be the bearer of the worst news imaginable.

When he was a younger man, he thought that informing someone that they were dying, or that they'd lost a loved one, was something that he would become hardened to, that would hurt him and sadden him less and less as time went on. But in fact, it only got worse. The older he got, the more he appreciated life, and the more tragic it seemed when someone lost it. Which is why he dedicated himself not only to saving lives as a doctor but to solving murders as an investigator.

On that day, at that moment, Dr. Mark Sloan was never more sure of his duty and his commitment to it. He would tell Billy Tidewell that his father was dead. And then he would find out why it happened. He would discover who killed Lydia Yates. And then he would make sure justice was finally done.

Billy Tidewell was in his bed, an IV tube

in his arm, staring at the ceiling when Mark came in.

"Hello, Billy," Mark said. "How are you feeling?"

"Tired, sore, bored, but not too bad for a guy who's been torn open," Billy said groggily. "Hey, did you bring me the tape?"

"What tape?" Mark asked.

"The UCLA game," Billy replied. "Dr. Travis said he'd tape it for me. I'm dying to know how it turned out. But if you know, don't ruin it for me."

He was going to ruin a lot more for him than that. Mark came up to the side of the bed, filled with dread. There was never any easy way to do this, never the right words to deliver the awful news and make it, somehow, less painful.

"How's Dad doing?" Billy asked. "I bet he's already on the phone screaming at suppliers."

"I'm afraid there were some unforeseen complications during surgery," Mark said somberly.

Billy stiffened, already anticipating the horrible news. How could it be anything less than horrible after an introduction like that? How could anyone not know what was coming?

"Billy," Mark said gently, "your father died."

Mark couldn't help watching, from the purely analytical perspective of a medical professional, how Billy took the news. Billy's eyes widened in shock. His mouth hung open. The blood seemed to drain from his face. His hands trembled slightly. All standard physiological and psychological reactions to traumatic news. There were other possible reactions, some more violent and extreme, all well-documented, all familiar to him. And yet, Mark's cold medical detachment only lasted for an instant. Unlike some other doctors, he couldn't sustain the distance; he couldn't help feeling the pain himself.

"No, it can't be," Billy stammered. "It's a routine operation; thousands are done every day. I don't understand."

"Neither do we, not yet," Mark said. "But there's an element of risk in every operation, particularly at his age and in his condition."

"But Dr. Stewart is one of the best, he's done hundreds of transplant surgeries," Billy said, his voice cracking. "He said it was routine. He said there would be no problem. He's never lost a patient. Never. How could he have let this happen?"

"I can assure you that Dr. Stewart and everyone on the surgical team did their very best," Mark said. "I'm very, very sorry."

Billy closed his eyes, squeezing out the tears that had been welling up. The tears rolled out of the corner of his eyes, dampening his pillow.

"Go," Billy whispered. "Just go."

Mark stood for a moment, in case Billy changed his mind, then walked away, unreasonably frustrated at his inability to ease his patient's obvious suffering. But this was the one kind of pain he was powerless to treat.

Steve brought home Chinese takeout, which they ate out on the deck while Mark filled him in on everything that had happened during the day.

After dinner, Steve asked to see the Lydia Yates file. Mark made them both a cup of coffee, sat down across from Steve at the kitchen table and gave him the file. Mark sipped his coffee and watched while his son opened up the file and began looking at the crime scene photos.

Steve studied the shots of Lydia Yates' body from every angle. He glanced at photos of the sewer pipe and the evidence, such as it was. All the items recovered in and around the pipe, from bottle caps to feces, were individually bagged and photographed. There were pictures of her car and everything in it, from particles on the floor mats to the items in her grocery bags. There were pictures of the shopping-center parking lot where her car was found and grainy stills taken from the surveillance cameras inside the Ralph's supermarket. Steve sorted through interviews with clerks and customers at the store, as well as Lydia's family, friends and co-workers.

After an hour, Steve closed the file, held his cup out to his father for a refill and sighed wearily. "There wasn't anything to go on three years ago. It will be even worse now."

Mark nodded sadly and poured them both some more coffee. "I know."

"I'll try to poke around discreetly, but word could get back to her family, and then we're going to be in trouble."

"*You'll* be in trouble, not me. There's nothing the chief can do to me if I look into the murder. The same isn't true for you," Mark said. "I appreciate what you're trying to do, but you should stay out of it. I don't want you jeopardizing your career for me."

"The last time I checked my job description, I got the distinct impression that I'm supposed to investigate homicides," Steve said. "This *is* a homicide, isn't it?"

"Yes, but the question is whether it's already been solved or not. I'm the only one who thinks it hasn't."

"No, you aren't. I'm going to investigate Lydia Yates' murder because that's my job, not yours. I'll keep you informed about whatever I find. Besides, you aren't going to have time to do all the tedious legwork anyway. You've got lots of files to read."

Mark nodded. "You mean the hundreds of boxes in the basement of Parker Center."

"Actually, I was thinking of the six boxes Amanda had me pick up for you from the medical examiner's office downtown."

Steve got up, trudged to the entry hall and returned with a large box, which he set on the kitchen table in front of his bewildered father.

"The others are in the garage," Steve said. "This one should keep you busy until I can find a hand truck."

Mark opened the box and looked inside. It was crammed with files. "What is all this?"

"The serial-killer cases you asked Tanis Archer to dig up," Steve said. "She couldn't get them without the chief finding out, and neither could I. So I took a different approach."

Now it was clear to Mark what Steve had done.

"You asked Amanda to get you whatever files the medical examiner's office might have," Mark said. "Great — now I've put her career at risk, too."

"She was glad to help out, Dad, though she had the same question I have. Why do you want to look at all these old cases?"

"It was something the chief said today. He was worried that if we raised questions about the Reaper killings it would encourage scrutiny of other cases where murders were credited to a serial killer that he either didn't confess to or wasn't prosecuted for."

"So you decided to make the chief's fear come true."

Mark shrugged.

"What do you hope to find?" Steve asked.

"Nothing," Mark said. "Absolutely nothing."

Ten miles away, alone in the darkness of her pathology lab, Amanda Bentley had exactly the same thought as Mark. She didn't want to find any evidence that suggested negligence or medical malpractice was the cause of Stanley Tidewell's death. She wanted it to be death by natural causes or a freak chain of events that led to a tragic accident. But all her experience and her instincts told her otherwise.

Amanda completed her autopsy, sent samples of blood and tissue to the lab for analysis, got a list of all the drugs given to Stanley before and during the operation and, finally, interviewed all the medical personnel involved in both the extraction and implantation of the kidney.

Now all that was left was what she was doing that night, sitting beside the corpse and correlating her own findings with the various test results as they came in. It was her job as chief of pathology to determine why this patient died. It was what she loved, being alone with the facts in the quiet lab, the only light the one shining over the body. Just her, a corpse and a death to explain.

But this death put her in a horribly awkward position, one she faced whenever the actions of any doctor at Community General might have contributed to the death of a patient. She knew the whole staff, respected most of them and hated to be the one who revealed their fatal mistakes. This was even worse. Amanda and Jack had been a team. They'd started out here together. And now his future was in her hands.

If she discovered he was responsible for Stanley's death, she wouldn't be his old, dear friend any more. She'd become the woman who destroyed his medical career and ruined his life. He would hate her forever. It would probably ruin her relationship with Mark, too. Mark would see her as the one who destroyed his protégé.

Why did Jack have to come back?

But Amanda couldn't let those feelings get in the way of her lonely work. They wouldn't change anything anyway. She was just the messenger. The body would speak for itself. All the facts, the entire story of what happened, was laid out in front of her on a slab, cut wide open. No longer a human being but flesh, organs, bones and fluids, microscopic molecules and strands of DNA. Scientific data to be analyzed and interpreted.

Feelings had nothing to do with it.

She went through the lab results and the chronology of events in the operating room one more time.

The body didn't lie.

Amanda knew the truth.

CHAPTER NINE

Lou Rozan and Freddy Meeks showed up at Mark's door at nine fifteen a.m., only forty-five minutes after he called them and asked them to come by. He told them it was urgent.

Mark greeted them wearing faded sweats and a ragged pair of slippers. His hair was disheveled, dark circles underscored his bloodshot eyes and his reading glasses were balanced on the tip of his nose.

"Thank you both for coming over. Please excuse the way I look and the mess you're about to see," Mark said, leading them into the house. "I've been working all night and haven't had a chance to clean up."

Crime scene photos, police reports, Post-it notes, a couple of Freddy's books and several yellow legal pads covered with Mark's handwritten scrawl were scattered all over the living room. Several boxes stamped with the medical examiner's insignia were stacked beside Mark's armchair.

Mark cleared a place on the sofa and motioned for them to sit down. He took a seat in the armchair facing them.

"What's this all about?" Freddy asked.

"I've been looking into some old serial killings," Mark said.

"Unsolved killings?" Lou asked.

Mark shifted in his seat. It wasn't the chair that was making him uncomfortable. "Yes and no."

"It's one or the other, Dr. Sloan."

"Yes, they're solved as far as the police, the courts and the public are concerned."

"But not you," Lou said.

"That would be the 'no' part he was alluding to," Freddy said.

"As you know, I believe Lydia Yates was killed by someone who wanted us to think the Reaper was responsible," Mark said. "That got me wondering. . . ."

"Uh-oh," Freddy said.

Mark patted the boxes stacked beside him. "These are files on a dozen California serial-killer cases going back ten years. The killers have all been captured, prosecuted and imprisoned, but not for all the murders they've been accused of. It's those unprosecuted murders that interest me."

He leaned forward and picked up a book off the floor. It was *Faces of Death* by

Freddy Meeks. The title and byline were boldly emblazoned above the snapshot of a dead French tourist lying in a trash-strewn alley, photographed by his killer.

"Like this one," Mark said, tapping the cover.

"That's Jean-Marc Gaddois, a tourist from Paris, killed in San Francisco by Randall Blore," Freddy said.

"Blore . . . yeah, I remember him," Lou said. "He was the guy who gunned down a dozen tourists and used a cantaloupe or an eggplant or something as a silencer."

"A potato," Mark said.

"Then he took pictures of his victims with their own cameras," Lou said, the details all coming back to him now. "What struck me as strange was that he left the pictures for us rather than taking them himself as trophies."

"What's so strange about that?" Freddy asked. "It was part of his plan. He wanted the pictures published all over the world to scare the hell out of any foreigner thinking of coming to visit. And it worked, too."

Mark remembered well that during Blore's six-month killing spree, foreign tourism to California sharply declined, bringing enormous pressure on law enforcement from the state capitol and irate business leaders. But it wasn't the police who ultimately captured Blore. He was caught by good Samaritans in Palm Springs after he shot a tourist. They chased him down and beat him nearly to death.

"Blore was prosecuted for three of the eleven murders police believe he's responsible for," Mark said. "I think he's guilty of all of them except his fifth kill, the French tourist."

"What makes that killing any different from the other ones?" Lou asked.

"On the surface, nothing," Mark replied. "But when you start examining the details, *everything*."

Mark laid out ten photos on the coffee table. They were unsettling still lifes of recent death. "Here are the pictures the killer took of his other victims. All of the shots are close-up portraits." He held up Freddy's book again. "But the picture of the French tourist is much wider and includes the trash and bits of potato around his body."

"That ain't much," Freddy said.

"But it got me thinking," Mark said. "If there's one difference, perhaps there's more. And there is. For starters, there's the bullet. The French tourist wasn't killed with the same gun used on the previous victims."

Freddy shook his head. "That's old news, Doc. Blore used at least three different weapons that we know of, and only one, the 357 Magnum he had on him when he was captured, was ever recovered. If the bullet is all you've got, you've been spinning your wheels for nothing."

"I found something far more significant than the bullet," Mark said. "There's the potato."

Lou looked at Mark incredulously. "The potato."

"Ninety-five percent of the potatoes sold in this country are stored and treated with chlorpropham, a postharvest sprout inhibitor," Mark said. "The potato used to silence the shot that killed Jean-Marc Gaddois had no traces of the chemical. It was an organic potato."

Lou sighed wearily. "Dr. Sloan, I mean no disrespect, but you're overthinking this. Just because one of the potatoes was organic doesn't prove a thing. It could be a fluke. I doubt Blores knew, or cared, whether his vegetable silencers were treated with chemicals or not."

Mark picked up a bulging file from the floor and spread out a stack of crime scene photos across the coffee table. They were various shots of obliterated potatoes, blown apart by gunblasts.

"What do you see?" he asked them.

"Potatoes," Lou said.

"Take a closer look."

"Little bitty chunks of potato," Freddy said, then pointed to another photo. "And some little bitty green chunks of potato."

"Exactly!" Mark said, pleased, waiting for them to see the rest. They didn't. His guests both looked at him quizzically. So he explained.

"Potatoes, like leaves, turn green after prolonged exposure to light. It's called greening, and gives potatoes an unpleasant, bitter taste," he said. "That's why merchants keep potatoes out of the light and throw away any that show the slightest bit of greening."

"What does this have to do with anything?" Lou asked, unable to completely hide the irritation from creeping into his voice. It was clear Lou thought this was all a waste of time. Mark expected that.

"The potatoes found at the other crime scenes showed little or no greening. This one was green," Mark explained. "Nobody would have sold it that way, which suggests the killer had the potato for some time, waiting for the opportunity to use it."

"So?" Lou asked.

"That's not the way Blore worked," Mark said. "He bought his potatoes an hour or so before his killings. He didn't keep his potatoes around for days."

Freddy stifled a small laugh. "I got to be honest here; I just don't understand why you're getting so worked up about a *potato*."

"Nothing about this potato matches the killings that came before or after the French tourist was murdered." Mark leaned forward to emphasize his point. "Why?"

"Why? Because shit happens," Freddy said. "I don't think it means anything."

"Neither do I," Lou said, staring at Mark. "But you're saying this proves someone else killed the French tourist and made it look like one of Blore's killings."

Mark leaned back in his chair again, finally satisfied. "Yes."

"And you're making this assumption based on a *potato*," Lou said in disbelief.

Mark pointed to Freddy's book on the coffee table. "And a picture of the French tourist that's taken from a wider angle than the pictures of the other victims."

"Okay," Lou said, "you're making this

assumption based on a snapshot *and* a potato."

"Yes."

Freddy and Lou shared a frustrated look. Freddy cleared his throat and tried to put what he was about to say as delicately as possible. "You don't see a problem with that."

"I see mistakes that reveal that whoever killed Jean-Marc Gaddois knew Blore's general M.O. but not the significant details."

Lou got up from the sofa. "It's all very interesting, Dr. Sloan, but we were expected downtown an hour ago."

"I found another one," Mark said.

"Excuse me?" Lou replied.

"Another questionable murder from a different serial killer case." Mark turned to Freddy. "You wrote about this killer, too. I think they even made a TV movie out of it." He scrounged around on the floor in the mess beside his chair until he found the other book. It was *The Traveler*. The cover depicted a lonely stretch of highway under dark, stormy skies.

Freddy groaned. "Doc, the Traveler confessed to all of the killings and a hundred more we don't know about."

"Which I'm sure came as a relief to who-

135

ever killed Jerry Ridling," Mark said. "Victim number nine."

Lou sighed and reluctantly sat down again. "The hitchhiker stabbed to death with an ice pick in Baker. Found in an empty swimming pool filled with trash."

"There's just one problem," Mark said.

"How did I know that was coming?" Freddy asked, shooting a glance at Lou.

"The time of death is pegged at around ten p.m.," Mark said. "But there is casino surveillance footage showing truck driver Tyler Cootes, the confessed serial killer, sitting at a blackjack table in Las Vegas at eleven forty-five the same night."

"Las Vegas is only about ninety miles away from Baker," Lou said. "That's plenty of time."

"If you're driving a hundred miles an hour the whole way. But a mile and a half east of Baker is the Halloran Summit, a gradual twenty-mile-long grade," Mark said. "Most cars can't muster much more than the speed limit along that stretch, so how did Cootes exceed it in his big rig towing a full load? The numbers just don't add up."

"Establishing time of death is not an exact science, Dr. Sloan," Lou said. "Especially when a body has been cooking in the

136

desert heat for two days."

"Even if you factor in an hour either way, the timing still doesn't work out," Mark said. "And I haven't even considered the time it took driving on city streets, parking his rig, walking across the lot and going into the casino."

"So you think someone killed Jerry Ridling and made it look like the Traveler did it," Freddy said. "Just like Lydia Yates and the French guy."

"I'm certain of it," Mark said. "I know you have your doubts, but assuming I'm right, how would you explain it?"

Freddy shrugged. "I can't, because the whole scenario doesn't make any sense to me."

Mark glanced at Lou. The ex-FBI profiler hesitated, meeting Mark's gaze. It was a challenge Lou didn't particularly want to confront. He knew that Mark already had a theory, and that by confirming Mark's suspicions, he'd be lending credibility to them, encouraging the doctor to continue his folly. Then again, there was probably no stopping Mark Sloan anyway.

"Either there are several murderers who've mimicked the crimes of serial killers," Lou said. "Or there's just one who has."

Mark nodded. "I believe there's a serial killer out there who has gone undetected all these years because all his victims look like victims of *another* killer."

"I don't buy it," Freddy said.

"Why not?" Mark asked.

"First off, because I don't believe you've proven those murders aren't the work of the killers they're attributed to. But that said, while a serial killer might want to hide his crimes, he ultimately wants attention for them. He would find some way to leave his mark; they all do, and I don't see it in any of these killings." Freddy looked Mark in the eye. "Do you?"

Mark shook his head. "Not yet."

"Not ever," Freddy said. He took out his pen, picked up *Faces of Death* from the coffee table and opened it to the title page. While Freddy scribbled something in the book, Mark turned to Lou.

"I know you have your doubts," Mark said. "But I think there's enough here to merit reopening these cases. I need you to go in with me to the chief and argue for an expansion of our mandate."

"You've been in the basement, Dr. Sloan. You've seen the hundreds of inactive files. Those are truly unsolved cases. They deserve our attention. All this," Lou said, sweeping his arm over the mess, "is a pointless distraction. I can't help you chase your tail on this."

"I can't either, Doc," Freddy said, though he hadn't been asked. "But I've autographed your book for you, so this meeting wasn't a total loss."

Freddy got up and handed Mark the book with a smile. Lou got up, too.

"Are you coming downtown?" Lou asked.

"I think I'll catch a nap first," Mark said. "I'm exhausted."

He walked them both to the door, thanked them again for coming and shuffled back into the living room. Mark couldn't blame them for being skeptical, but while explaining the facts to them, he'd thoroughly convinced himself that an unusually devious serial killer had fooled them all for years.

Mark opened *Faces of Death* and read Freddy's inscription. *I'm glad you're buying my books. I just wish you'd stop trying to rewrite them! Your friend, Freddy Meeks.*

He smiled and tossed the book on the floor amidst all the photos, files and papers. Lou was right about one thing. Mark's first responsibility was to those unsolved cases gathering dust in the LAPD basement. Whatever Mark thought he'd found could wait for a few more weeks, at least until he'd fulfilled his obligation to the task force.

He started to walk away, then turned back again. Something wasn't right. He let his gaze pass over the mess in the room, but his eyes kept coming back to Freddy's book. What was it about the book? Or was it the picture?

It couldn't be the picture. Mark already knew what was bothering him about that. The corpse was photographed from a wider angle than the other tourists who were killed.

Why had the killer done that? To show us more of the body? Or to show us something else?

Mark squatted over the book, looking at the cover, but he didn't see anything he hadn't seen before. A dead body. A trash-strewn alley. No different from the other tourist killings. No different from the killings of the Reaper or the Traveler.

No different.

Mark scrambled on his hands and knees around the living room, sorting through the mess for the crime scene photos of Lydia Yates and Jerry Ridling. Lydia in the sewage pipe. Jerry in the garbage at the bottom of the empty pool. He gathered the photos together and laid them out beside Freddy's book, the photo of Jean-Marc Gaddois lying in the filthy alley.

And then he saw it. He saw what the killer wanted him to see in the picture of the French tourist. The same thing he now saw in the pictures of Lydia Yates and Jerry Ridling.

He saw the killer's signature.

CHAPTER TEN

Mark rushed out of the house so quickly, he left his beeper and cell phone behind. He was already on the Santa Monica Freeway heading to the UCLA Department of Mathematics when his beeper started trilling, and then his cell phone began ringing, both going unheard in his empty house.

The calls and pages were from Amanda. She finally gave up trying to reach him. He would have to find out what she'd discovered later. Officially, she didn't need him at the hospital for this. She was authorized and, in fact, expected, to inform the doctors involved of her determination. Unofficially, she was afraid to go through it alone. She wanted Mark there for support. Not just for her, but for all of them.

But she couldn't delay her findings any longer. It wasn't fair to Stanley Tidewell's family, the hospital or the doctors involved. Jack and Jesse. Her friends.

She called Jack and Jesse and told them to come to the pathology lab in an hour.

The two doctors showed up a half hour early. She'd known they would. Jesse was quiet, almost sullen. Jack was the opposite, filled with nervous energy, unable to stop smiling, though he certainly wasn't happy.

Amanda took a deep breath and flipped through her papers, though it was just a way to avoid looking at Jack. She didn't need notes to remind her of what she'd discovered.

"My autopsy on Mr. Tidewell revealed extensive pulmonary and laryngeal edema, which led to a dramatic drop in blood pressure, bronchospasm and cardiac arrest," she said, eyes still on her report. "My determination is that he died of anaphylaxis."

"A severe allergic reaction?" Jack asked skeptically. "That's not possible."

Amanda glanced at Jack. She couldn't do this hiding from him any longer. "You gave Mr. Tidewell a presurgical antibiotic, Jack."

"That's standard," Jack said.

"Do you remember what you gave him?" Amanda asked.

"Yeah, of course," Jack said. "Cephalosporin, one gram IV."

Jesse groaned and shook his head, his face rigid with anger.

Jack looked quizzically at Jesse, then back to Amanda. "What am I not getting here?"

"I'll tell you," Jesse said quietly, trying to suppress his rage. "If you'd spent two seconds reading Mr. Tidewell's file, he'd still be alive; that's what you're 'not getting here.' "

"Jesse," Amanda said. "Please."

"But no," Jesse seethed, "you were more interested in the football game you were missing."

"That's enough!" Amanda shouted, rising from her seat.

"You killed him, hotshot." Jesse pointed at Jack. "Think about that while you're waxing your SL."

Jesse marched out, slamming the door behind him. After a moment, Jack turned and faced Amanda.

"Is he right?" he asked, though he already knew the answer from the grave expression on her face.

"Mr. Tidewell was allergic to penicillin," Amanda said.

"I didn't give him penicillin."

"You gave him a pre-op injection of cephalosporin," she said. "Chemically, they are very close. There's a severe risk of cross-reactivity. People allergic to penicillin can experience the same symptoms from the antibiotic."

Jack sat down slowly in the chair across from Amanda. "Oh my God."

"It was an accident, Jack," Amanda said softly.

"It was negligence," he said.

"The hospital review committee hasn't even examined the case yet," Amanda said. "They'll decide if there was any negligence involved."

"I've decided." Jack looked at her, studied her face for a moment, then shook his head sadly. "And so have you."

LAPD Police Chief John Masters sat behind his massive desk while Mark Sloan rambled on and on about photos of dead people, discrepancies in time and potatoes. Lots of stuff about potatoes. Masters was only half-listening now, thinking instead about what a mistake it had been to appoint Mark Sloan to his task force.

The gist of Mark's yammering, as far as Masters was concerned, was that Mark had defied his orders and continued nosing around in serial-killer cases that had long since been solved.

The chief couldn't do much to Mark, but he could certainly punish those who had helped him. Mark didn't get those confidential police files using a transporter beam. Steve Sloan had certainly aided and abetted his father. Too often Steve had put family loyalty above loyalty to the department. Perhaps a demotion in rank would make him think twice the next time his dad asked for a favor.

What was he thinking, appointing Mark Sloan to the task force?

The chief couldn't possibly have foreseen the misplaced file and the trouble it would cause. But he certainly could have foreseen the trouble. With the doctor, it was inevitable. The chief had hoped his stern lecture the other day would dissuade Mark and the task force from straying into areas that were none of their concern. But when had he *ever* been able to keep Mark Sloan away from anything that didn't concern him?

Now, here Mark was, in a rumpled sport coat and looking like he just crawled out of bed, ranting like a madman. Enough was enough. Masters held his hand up, palm out to Mark, stopping the doctor midsentence.

"Dr. Sloan, you barged in here saying you had news that couldn't wait, that lives were at stake. That was quite a while ago and I still haven't heard anything that merits my attention."

Mark bristled with anger, something he could have controlled if he wasn't so tired. "You haven't heard a word I've said."

"On the contrary, Doctor. I've heard you loud and clear. I appointed you to a task force on unsolved crimes. Instead, you've taken it upon yourself to reinvestigate serial killers who have already been apprehended and punished."

"And one who hasn't, the one who murdered Lydia Yates, Jerry Ridling and Jean-Marc Gaddois," Mark said. "He has eluded detection for years by making his killings look as if another serial killer did them. Who knows how many other murders he's responsible for?"

"Even if I was persuaded by your argument, which I am not, you haven't shown me anything that proves a connection between the three victims."

"I was just getting to that."

Mark turned his back to Masters and rooted around in the large gym bag he'd brought along to carry everything he wanted to show the chief. While he did, Masters wondered why he'd let Mark into his office, why he was even listening to what he had to say. Mark Sloan wasn't a cop, or an elected official, or a community leader, or even one of those know-nothing citizens on the police commission. He was just an irritating busybody who happened to have a son on the force. The chief had inherited this relationship with Mark Sloan from his ineffectual predecessors. The whole point of putting Mark on the task force was to co-opt him, not empower him.

Mark found the crime scene photos of the dead tourists and laid them out on the desk in front of the chief.

"All the other pictures of the tourists were close-up portraits, but this one of the French tourist is taken from a distance," Mark said, pointing to the picture that had been reproduced on Meeks' book jacket. "I asked myself, what did he want us to see?"

Master glanced at the picture of the French tourist. "All I see is a corpse and the filth on the ground."

"Precisely," Mark said. "The body is surrounded by trash. With just the naked eye, we can clearly see a wad of dried gum, a bottle cap, a patch of grease, scraps of old newspaper."

Mark scooped up the pictures of all the tourists except Gaddois, replacing them on the desk with crime scene photos of Lydia Yates and Jerry Ridling.

"Lydia Yates was found in a sewer, Jerry Ridling in an empty swimming pool," Mark said. "They were both surrounded by trash, too. That's the link."

"The trash?"

"One particular piece of trash," Mark said. "A bottle cap."

Mark whipped a magnifying glass out from his jacket and offered it to the chief, who looked at him a moment, wondering if the doctor also had a deerstalker cap and meerschaum pipe at home, too.

Masters took the magnifying glass and studied the picture with it while Mark continued talking.

"An Oakes Diet Root Beer bottle cap was found at the scene of each murder," Mark said. "No one noticed it. So when the killer took the picture of the French tourist, he made sure to include the bottle cap. He did everything except draw a circle around it for us, and we still missed it."

The chief set the magnifying glass down, leaned back in his chair and glowered at Mark. "I still don't see any connection."

"The same bottle cap is at every crime scene," Mark said emphatically.

"It's a coincidence," the chief said. "You could probably find the same bottle cap in just about every trash bin in this city."

"Actually, you're wrong about that," Mark replied. "Oakes is a small regional brand, based in Temecula. Very few grocery stores carry it; even fewer stock the diet line. And Oakes products aren't available at all in Baker. The odds of finding an Oakes Diet Root Beer bottle cap at all three crime scenes, in three different corners of the state, are astronomical. In fact, I took the liberty of contacting a mathematics professor at UCLA and asked him to calculate the odds for me."

Mark rummaged in his gym bag and hurriedly retrieved a thick printout. But in his haste, he picked the stack up from the sides rather than from the bottom, so when he turned to hand the report to the Chief, he accidentally unfurled the huge printout in a stream of paper behind him.

As the chief watched disdainfully, Mark tried to gather up the unfurled mess as he continued to make his argument. "The professor factored in the number of bottles sold each year, the number of grocery stores in which they are sold, along with the population figures for the state of California, then correlated that against the total number of all brands of soft drinks sold in —"

Mark stopped, realizing that all he'd

managed to do was tangle himself up in the continuous printout. Finally, in frustration, Mark simply tore the paper, rolled it up into a massive ball, and piled it onto one of the two seats facing the chief's desk. Then, exhausted, Mark sat in the other chair across from Masters.

"I won't bore you with all the figures now," said Mark, motioning to the mound of crumpled paper. "You can review them at your leisure."

The chief just stared at him. He saw a pathetic old man who was, quite possibly, slipping headlong into dementia. "That won't be necessary, Doctor. I've heard enough."

Mark nodded, pleased. "We should begin by looking at every serial-killing case in L.A. over the last twenty years to see if that bottle cap has turned up at any other crime scene, then —"

"We will do no such thing," the chief interrupted. "We won't help you pursue your delusions any further."

"There's a serial killer out there who has been murdering people with impunity for years."

"There are people who look at satellite photos of simple rock formations on Mars and see ruins of a fallen statue. You look at potatoes and bottle caps and see serial killers." The chief sighed. "It's sad and more than a little disturbing."

"You've solved homicides based on facts and assumptions derived from carpet fibers, flecks of dirt, bread crumbs, fingernail clippings, ink stains and stray hairs," Mark said. "This is no different. I am making reasonable deductions based on physical evidence found at multiple crime scenes. That evidence reveals the presence of a serial killer at work. If you don't take action, he'll just keep on killing. He has to be stopped."

"The only one who has to be stopped is you, Dr. Sloan, before you do anything more serious than simply embarrass yourself," the chief said. "I am removing you from the task force, effective immediately. You will no longer be allowed in this building unescorted."

The chief gathered up all the photos on his desk and stuck them in his drawer. "You were only authorized to look at the unsolved case files. I did not give you blanket permission to ransack our files, nor did I give anyone else the authority to do it for you. I will be sending officers to your home for all the confidential files in your possession. They are stolen property. You are to turn them over to me immediately or I will have you arrested. Do I make myself clear?"

"Perfectly. You're so afraid of political fallout that you would rather let a murderer keep on killing than do your job," Mark said. "Maybe you can live with that, but I can't."

The chief rose from his seat and towered over Mark. "A word of advice, Dr. Sloan. You don't want me as an adversary. It will come out badly for both you and your son."

Mark wasn't intimidated. Threats had the opposite effect on him. They only reinforced his commitment. He got up slowly and looked Masters in the eye. "A lot of police chiefs have come and gone in this city, but I'm still here, doing what I've always done. That should tell you something."

He picked up his gym bag and walked out, the chief glaring after him.

CHAPTER ELEVEN

Lonnie Milton, the placement coordinator in the valley office of Staff Genius Temporary Services, had the vacant-eyed expression of a man who knew with dull certainty that all his tomorrows would be just like today.

Lonnie wore the standard uniform of a thirty-year-old office worker who can only afford to shop at the Gap: khaki pants, white shirt, navy blue blazer — all slightly wrinkled.

His job was to place temporary workers in short-term clerical positions at offices throughout the San Fernando Valley. One of his regular clients had been Lydia Yates, which is why Steve Sloan sat across from him, his little notebook open, ballpoint pen poised to take copious notes. So far, all he had written was Lonnie's name, which he'd put a box around. Steve was working on giving the box some shadows to add a 3-D effect.

"She was a hard worker, well liked, always busy," Lonnie said in his flat monotone. "Efficient, fast and trustworthy."

"Did any individual employer show an unusual interest in her, maybe ask you for details about her personal life, like her home address or phone number?"

"It's against company policy to give that information out."

"But did anyone ask for it?"

"No."

"Did she have any troubles at work?" Steve asked. Lonnie struck him as the kind of guy who might show up at work one day with an AK-47 just for the change of pace.

"What kind of troubles?" Lonnie asked.

"A coworker making inappropriate advances, something like that?" Steve glanced at Lonnie's paperwork on the desk. He was doodling on Steve's card. Putting a box around his name and adding shadows for depth. Steve abruptly snapped his notebook closed and realized with a pang of nausea that this guy probably still lived at home, too.

"No," Lonnie said.

"What about you?" Steve asked. "Did you ever go out with her?"

"No."

"Did she turn you down?"

"I didn't ask," Lonnie said. "She wasn't my type."

"What type is that?" *The kind that doesn't mind guys who live with their parents,* Steve thought, with a tinge of embarrassment.

"The type who isn't efficient, fast and trustworthy," Lonnie said. "Besides, it's against company policy to fraternize with the clients."

Lonnie's phone rang. He snatched it up and answered, "Staff Genius Temporary Services; Lonnie Milton speaking; how may we help you make your day more productive?" His voice had the flat quality of a recording. If he hit a key on the phone for a beep-tone, Steve thought, nobody would know the difference. Lonnie held the phone out to Steve. "It's for you."

The news came as quite a shock to Steve, considering he hadn't told anybody where he was going to be and who he was going to see.

Steve took the receiver. "Yeah?"

"Wise choice starting your investigation of Lydia Yates at Staff Genius. You may be needing their services very soon yourself." It was the unmistakable voice of LAPD Police Chief John Masters. "Be in my office in one hour, Detective."

The chief hung up. *At least I'm still a de-*

tective, Steve thought.

Mark was asleep, fully clothed, on top of his bed when he was awakened by the insistent knocking on his front door. He glanced at the clock radio beside the bed. It was four o'clock in the afternoon. He'd been napping for only a couple of hours, but that was still longer than he'd intended.

It wasn't unusual for him to work through the night, driven by fierce curiosity and a surge of adrenaline, but lately he felt the fatigue in a way he never had before. He knew it was his age, but he simply refused to accept it. Mark expected his body to keep up with his mind, to function the same way it did when he was twenty-five years old, when he could easily go a day or more without sleep.

Of course, two hours of hard labor in the midday sun when he got home from seeing the chief didn't help his stamina, either.

Mark got up, trudged barefoot to the entry hall and saw Jack standing on the porch, shifting his weight nervously from foot to foot.

"Jack, what are you doing here?" Mark said as he opened the door.

"I couldn't do this on the phone," Jack

said. "May I come in?"

"Of course." Mark stepped aside and let Jack pass. "Can I get you some coffee or something?"

"No, thanks."

Jack stood in the center of Mark's living room, which showed no signs of its earlier disarray, with the exception of Freddy's books, which were now back in their place on the bookshelf. All the files were gone, and so were the boxes from the medical examiner's office.

"Look, Mark, you can drop the act."

"What act?" Mark asked, genuinely puzzled.

"I know how disappointed you must be in me," Jack said, full of shame. "I want you to know how sorry I am."

"Jack, you have nothing to apologize for."

"You had faith in me when no one else did. You taught me everything you knew and treated me like a member of your family," Jack said. "How did I repay you? By becoming cocky, rich and sloppy. By killing your patient in your hospital. What a guy I am."

"It's a little early to be crucifying yourself," Mark said with a reassuring smile. "We don't know what happened to Stanley yet. It may turn out that his death had nothing to do with you."

Jack turned slowly to face him. "You haven't heard?"

"I'm afraid I was preoccupied with something else," Mark said, apologetic. "Did Amanda come up with something?"

"She discovered that Stanley died at the hands of an incompetent doctor," Jack said. "Stanley was allergic to penicillin."

"You didn't give him any penicillin," Mark said, puzzled.

"But I ordered a pre-op injection of cephalosporin," Jack said heavily.

Mark reacted as if he'd sustained a physical blow. He stared at Jack in astonishment.

"I've done it a thousand times with a thousand transplant patients," Jack said. "I did it without thinking. Without looking at his chart."

Jack glanced at Mark, who still seemed to be reeling from the news. It only made Jack feel guiltier.

"I won't let my mistake reflect badly on you, I promise," Jack said in a rush, eager to regain some measure of Mark's respect. "I'll take full responsibility when the hospital's Morbidity and Mortality Review Committee convenes next week. I'll do the same when this comes up before the state medical board."

"You won't have to," Mark said firmly, with no trace of anger or disappointment in his voice. "You didn't do anything wrong."

"I gave him the antibiotic, Mark."

"You may have given him the antibiotic," Mark said, "but I can assure you that wasn't what killed Stanley."

"How do you know?"

"Because it didn't kill him when I gave him the same antibiotic three months ago," Mark said.

Now it was Jack's turn to be shocked. Jack didn't know which was more unbelievable, that he hadn't killed Stanley after all or that Mark had made the same deadly mistake he had.

"You couldn't have," Jack stammered.

"Stanley came in with a kidney infection. I treated him with cephalosporin," Mark said. "I didn't consider his allergy to penicillin. I made an error that could have had tragic consequences. But it didn't. Stanley responded well to the treatment and was just fine. I didn't see Stanley again until he checked himself in for the transplant."

Jack sat down in Mark's armchair. "This doesn't make any sense."

"There's a risk that people allergic to penicillin will have the same reaction to cephalosporin, but it's not a certainty. He was lucky or I might have killed him three months ago," Mark hunted around for his shoes and found them under the coffee table. They were covered with sand.

"All doctors make mistakes, Jack. Me included. That doesn't make us incompetent or negligent; it just proves we're human and as fallible as anybody else." Mark took his shoes out on the deck, clapped them together, then sat back down on the couch to put them on. "Unfortunately, when we make mistakes, people can die."

"Then if it wasn't the antibiotic that killed Stanley, what did?"

"That's what we're going to find out," Mark said, getting up. "We'll start by taking a closer look at the body."

Mark and Jack were already heading towards the entry hall when the doorbell rang. Detective Tanis Archer and a half dozen uniformed police officers were standing outside. Mark opened the door.

Tanis greeted him with a pained expression on her face. "I've got a search warrant, Dr. Sloan. The chief wants those files." She handed over the warrant to Mark, who took a quick glance at it, then

161

motioned them inside.

"I'm on my way out," Mark said, "so please lock up when you leave."

The officers filed into the house, leaving Tanis alone on the doorstep with Mark and Jack.

"You could make it easy on me and just tell me where they are," Tanis said.

"Who said I had any files?" Mark handed the search warrant back to Tanis.

"Those crime scene photos you showed the chief today came from somewhere."

"You know my hobby is magic," Mark said, smiling mischievously.

"I'm sure you're especially good at making things disappear," said Tanis, and then muttered something only he could hear as she passed by him.

"You better be," she whispered.

Steve made it down to Parker Center in thirty-five minutes, then sat in the parking lot for another fifteen running through scenarios of what might be awaiting him. He'd defied the chief, and Masters could express his wrath in any number of unpleasant ways. A reprimand. A suspension. Reassignment. Or outright dismissal from the force.

No matter how Steve looked at it, this

wasn't going to be a good meeting. He should have brought a dozen Krispy Kremes as a peace offering, start the meeting off on a pleasant note. Who can fire someone who just delivered hot donuts?

He wasn't surprised Masters had found him at Staff Genius. The chief had been a crack homicide detective himself and could easily guess where Steve would start his investigation. Nor was he surprised that the chief called him on the Staff Genius phone rather than on his cell. The chief was a shrewd politician and gamesman; he knew the power of dramatic effect.

Steve wondered if Staff Genius hired security guards. An ex-cop could probably scratch out a decent living between doing event security at concerts and sitting in the guard shack at one of those gated communities in the valley. He checked his watch. He couldn't put it off any longer.

The first thing Steve noticed when he entered the chief's huge, corner office wasn't the expansive view of downtown Los Angeles, the many awards or citations decorating the walls or even Masters' stony gaze. It was the massive computer printout, gathered together into a big ball and stuffed between the armrests of one the chief's guest chairs. In that instant, Steve knew with absolute certainty that his father had been there. Who else would have left such a mess? And why else would the chief have left it there for him to see?

"Your father has embarked on a dangerous escapade," the chief said, speaking in an even tone.

"Dangerous for whom?" Steve asked.

"This entire city. If he continues to pursue this obsession of his, he will cast doubt on dozens of hard-won convictions, whip up a media frenzy and maybe end up putting dozens of convicted killers back on the streets." The chief studied Steve, who stood in front of his desk. "And you'd help him do all that, wouldn't you?"

"If I thought he was right," Steve said, "which he usually is."

The chief mulled that over for a moment, then spoke in a voice so low Steve almost didn't hear it.

"Who do you work for?" Masters asked. "Him or me?"

"You."

The chief got out of his seat and went to the window, taking in the view of his city, his back to Steve. "But you'll follow his lead over mine."

"He's my father."

The chief nodded. "He has no police training. He hasn't got a badge. He has no formal experience in homicide investigation."

"And he's better at it than any cop on this force."

The chief turned, a scornful smile on his face. "Including you?"

"Yeah," Steve said. "Including me."

The chief approached Steve, standing just a few inches away from him. He liked to use his physical superiority to intimidate people, to intrude on their personal space. It forced them to look up at him, to feel small and vulnerable. With most people it worked. It certainly worked with Steve, who liked to use the same technique on people and wasn't comfortable having the tables turned.

"I've always wondered something," the chief said, peering down at Steve like a bug. "How does it feel having your father constantly intrude in your work, second-guessing every move you make, proving you wrong all the time?"

It wasn't as though Steve hadn't been asked that question before, though never quite as bluntly.

Although Steve moved quickly up the LAPD ranks, the popular wisdom was that

Mark Sloan solved the cases and Steve simply stepped in to make the arrests. For those difficult, seemingly impossible cases, the popular wisdom was largely true. But those brain-twister cases were a small percentage of the police work Steve did on a regular basis. Working those day-to-day cases, the constant trickle of drive-by shootings, deadly holdups and fatal domestic squabbles, Steve had proved to be a competent, hardworking and dogged investigator.

But those weren't the homicides that got noticed, certainly not by the media or the departmental hierarchy. Steve's own accomplishments, which were considerable, were largely lost in the media glare and headlines that followed his father's high-profile successes.

Steve could tolerate the jeers and jibes from his coworkers, who teased him mercilessly about his father always showing up at his crime scenes. He could even handle being ignored while his father enjoyed all the acclaim and respect.

What tortured Steve was how easily he could be misled by the evidence, while his father rarely was. How Steve's instincts could be so wrong while his father's intuition was almost always right. Over the years, the resentment built up so much, Steve began to wonder if solving cases was what his father really enjoyed, or if it was making a fool out of his son.

But a couple of years ago, Steve asked himself if he resented it so much, if it was such a burden, why didn't he move to another city? Join a different department? Make a life and a career for himself far away from his father's shadow?

The answers weren't hard to find, and it didn't take a shrink or a dozen self-help books to dredge them up. Just a few morning runs around the track to sweat them out.

He stayed, he put up with it all, because he loved his father. Because his father had an amazing gift for unraveling puzzles, whether it was the Sunday crossword or a multiple homicide. Because he admired his father more than anyone else. Because Steve was a far better detective with his father than without him.

Once Steve accepted that, he made some fundamental changes in his philosophy towards his father in general and police work in specific.

Steve stopped fighting with his dad, stopped questioning his instincts and deductions. Instead, he used his police training and street experience to complement his father's natural abilities. He began seeking out his dad's advice instead of waiting for it to be offered. He tried to understand his father's reasoning, to see if there were techniques he could apply to problems himself. He even accepted his father's offer to share the beach house with him.

Suddenly, everything changed. Steve became even more successful at closing homicides than he was before. And the perception of Steve within the department began to change as well, though apparently not with Chief Masters.

So when the chief asked Steve how it felt to be overshadowed by his dad, it wasn't the raw nerve Masters thought, or perhaps hoped, it would be. Steve had made peace with it long ago.

Steve smiled up at the chief. "I welcome his involvement. And if you're smart, sir, so should you."

The rest of the meeting went downhill from there, and thirty minutes later, Steve left the chief's office, his ears still ringing. He stepped into the elevator, which was already occupied by two uniformed cops. As soon as they saw Steve, they shared amused grins.

"Say, Buck," one officer said to the other, looking at Steve as he spoke. "You see that lady cop in vice any more?"

"Sweet Caroline?" Buck answered, also looking at Steve, as if to make sure he was listening. It was hard not to in an elevator.

"Yeah, her. Bet the two of you made some *beautiful noise* together."

Sweet Caroline. Beautiful noise. It could be a coincidence, Steve thought nervously. *There's no way they could know. . . .*

"She was great company on a *hot August night,*" that's for sure," Buck said, stifling a laugh.

"I loved the way she dressed," the other cop said, also trying hard not to break up. "Seemed like she was *forever in blue jeans.*"

Oh my God, Steve thought. *They knew.* Steve felt a flush of embarrassment rising on his face. How could they know?

"What happened between you two?" the cop asked Buck, like Abbott lobbing a straight line at Costello.

"What can I say? Our *love is on the rocks,*" Buck said, and the two cops lost it completely, doubling over in gales of laughter.

"Very funny," Steve hissed. There was only one way they could have discovered his secret. Probably the whole department knew by now, and a lot more embarrassing

169

things about him, too. The elevator stopped at the lobby and Steve marched out.

"Don't forget to *turn on your heartlight!*" Buck yelled after him, and the two officers collapsed into laughter all over again.

Mark called Amanda on his cell phone on his way to the hospital with Jack. Amanda immediately ordered a new screening of Stanley's blood and internal organs, then laid out the corpse for reexamination.

While they waited for the lab results, the three doctors conducted what amounted to a second autopsy. Mark had to see the body for himself, to be certain he agreed with Amanda's findings. Jack needed to review his work, to convince himself that he hadn't done anything wrong during the transplant procedure itself. And Amanda, in light of the new information, wanted to double-check her own work.

All three of them came away satisfied. Mark agreed that the physical evidence supported Amanda's finding of anaphylaxis, and Jack was confident that no surgical errors were made during the transplant. In fact, from what Mark could see, Jack and Amanda had both done exemplary work.

So if Jack hadn't made a mistake, and if

Amanda's findings were correct, what had gone wrong? What caused the profound allergic reaction that led to Stanley's sudden death?

An assistant brought Amanda the new lab report. She quickly scanned the document, speaking up as soon as she hit a relevant fact. "The blood test came up negative for penicillin."

"That can't be," Jack said, throwing his hands up in desperation. "There are only two other things we know Stanley Tidewell was allergic to — high-SPF sunscreen and fleabites. I didn't slather him with Coppertone and we weren't attacked by a swarm of fleas."

"Hold on, Jack. I only said there wasn't any penicillin in his blood." Amanda looked up from the report, stunned. "But his kidney was saturated with it."

Jack didn't know what to make of the revelation at first, so he turned to Mark, who had a strange, contemplative look on his face.

"Very interesting," Mark said, his voice trailing off with his thoughts.

"It's a hell of a lot more than that," Jack said, relieved. "It means I'm in the clear."

"And it raises a lot more questions," Amanda said.

"Yeah, like why didn't you find this before?" Jack asked, instantly regretting the accusatory tone in his voice.

"Because she didn't look for it," Mark said, sounding a bit distracted, his mind still working on something. "I wouldn't have, either."

"Why not?" Jack asked.

"Because everything added up," Mark said, suddenly focused, a strange smile on his face. Both Jack and Amanda had seen it a million times before. It meant Mark was on to something.

"Stanley died of a severe allergic reaction," Mark said. "A review of his medical file shows he was allergic to penicillin. The postmortem lab results didn't show any in his blood. But the record of the transplant operation indicates you gave him a cephalosporin IV, which can provoke the same deadly anaphylactic reaction. The cause of death is obvious. It's open and shut."

"Obviously not," Amanda said remorsefully. "If I'd done my job right the first time, this never would have happened. I should have tested the kidney." She turned to Jack. "I am so sorry for putting you through all this."

"Like Mark said, you had no reason to

172

check the kidney for penicillin," Jack said. "I don't blame you for anything and you certainly don't owe me any apologies."

Mark nodded in agreement. "Any pathologist would have done exactly what you did and would have reached the same conclusion," he said. "In fact, the murderer was counting on it."

"*Murderer?*" Jack exclaimed. "What murderer?" He looked at Amanda, who looked at Mark.

"There was a murderer?" she asked.

"Of course; isn't it obvious?" Mark replied, then saw from the expressions on their faces that apparently it wasn't. "The kidney was saturated with penicillin, yet there was no penicillin in Stanley's blood. That's because the anaphylactic reaction didn't begin until the instant his blood began to flow through the new kidney. The antigen, in this case the penicillin molecules, reacted with the antibodies in his blood, creating powerful chemicals that swept throughout his body in seconds. He was dead before the penicillin could get into his bloodstream."

Amanda and Jack could almost hear Mark's mind working, beeping and booping and binging like one of those early supercomputers, spools of tape spinning,

173

thousands of lights flashing.

"There's only one way this could have happened." Mark looked down at Stanley's open belly. "At some point during the operation, between the moment the kidney was harvested and when it was implanted, someone tainted the organ with penicillin." Mark looked up again at them. "This was murder."

Jack shook his head. "A visit to Los Angeles to see Mark Sloan just wouldn't be complete without hearing those three words."

"You know what this means?" Amanda considered the facts for a moment. "Either someone in the operating room really hated Stanley Tidewell or," she glanced at Jack, "someone really hated *you*."

CHAPTER TWELVE

There were only a couple of cars in the parking lot in front of BBQ Bob's when Jesse pulled in. Even so, he parked a good distance from the front door. He wanted to make sure the customers got the best spots.

Jesse had come straight to the restaurant after his shift at the hospital. A lot of people wondered how, and why, he tried to balance two jobs. But working at BBQ Bob's wasn't a whole lot different from going back to his apartment, except here he actually had to keep the kitchen and bathrooms clean.

He was lost in thought, so he wasn't aware of Jack getting out of the rented Explorer he'd just passed.

"Hey, sport," Jack called from behind.

Jesse turned and stepped right into Jack's right hook. He took it in the mouth and hit the ground hard. Jack stood over him, red-faced with fury, pointing a finger down at him as he spoke.

"You want a piece of me, you coward,

you come and get it," Jack hissed. "You don't hurt innocent people."

Jesse blinked hard, trying to bring the number of Jacks he saw down to just one. "What the hell are you talking about?" he sputtered, barely audible, blood in his spittle.

Jack stepped closer because he didn't want Jesse to miss a word. "You tainted Stanley's kidney with penicillin and killed him just to ruin me."

Jesse suddenly scissored his legs, catching Jack's ankles and yanking them out from under him. As Jack went down, Jesse sprang up, kicking Jack hard in the gut.

"You think I'd kill a guy over you?" Jesse grabbed Jack by the arm, yanked it behind Jack's back and lifted the doctor to his feet. He put his mouth close to Jack's ear and gave Jack's arm a painful upward pull.

"You're nothing to me," Jesse said. "Same as you are to Mark and Amanda, or were you too busy looking at yourself in the mirror to notice?"

Jack let out a warlike yelp and hurled himself backwards into his Explorer, bashing Jesse hard against the driver's side window, shattering the glass. Stunned, Jesse inadvertently released Jack, who spun around and jammed his forearm across Jesse's throat, pinning him against the car.

"Wasn't just me you wanted, was it?" Jack said, practically spitting into Jesse's grimacing face. "I saw the sign across the street. 'Burger Beach coming soon.' You're as bad a murderer as you are a doctor."

Jesse kneed Jack in the groin and tried to put him in a headlock. But Jack recovered faster than Jesse anticipated, grabbed Jesse's wrist and twisted. Jesse cried out and lost his balance but managed to grab Jack's free arm and pin it behind his back. Both men hit the pavement, wrapped around each other like a human pretzel, each man trapping the other in a painful hold, neither able to look the other in the eye. In fact, neither of them was exactly sure who had the advantage or how to make the best use of it.

"You think I'd intentionally kill my own patient out of pride and greed?" Jesse grunted between gritted teeth.

"Hell, yes," Jack managed to croak, grimacing in anger and frustration.

"You think I'd do that to Mark? To Amanda? To Steve?" Jesse said, giving Jack's arm a good yank. Jack yelped. "Would you?"

"No," Jack hissed.

Jesse released Jack, who then released him. They untangled themselves from each other and lay on their backs on the pavement, breathing hard, bloody and exhausted.

"Where did you learn to fight like that?" Jack asked.

"My dad."

"He a wrestler or something?"

"He's a spy," Jesse replied.

Jack began to laugh, and Jesse did too, without even knowing why.

"What's so funny about that?" Jesse asked.

"Your dad's a secret agent?"

"Yeah."

"Nobody's dad is a secret agent," Jack said.

"Nobody's dad is a mobster," Jesse replied.

"My dad is."

"There you go," Jesse said. "Guess neither one of us is for real."

They both lay there on the ground for a moment, catching their breath. That's when they both became aware of a man standing at their feet, looking down at them. It was a guy with bad skin wearing a miniheadset, listening to the music on the MP3 player clipped to his belt. He had two bulging manila envelopes under one of his scrawny arms.

"One of you guys Jack Stewart?" the kid asked, bouncing to the beat of his music.

"Yeah," Jack said.

The guy looked at Jesse. "Are you Jesse Travis?"

"That's me," Jesse said.

"Cool." The kid dropped one heavy envelope beside each of them. "Consider yourselves served," he said, and rolled away on a pair of skate sneakers, just like the kind Mark wore.

Jack propped himself up on an elbow, opened the flap of the envelope and pulled out the sheaf of legal papers inside. He groaned.

"Billy Tidewell is suing me for thirty million dollars for wrongful death and medical malpractice," Jack said. "You, too, by the way, and Community General Hospital."

"Dandy." Jesse got up, grunting with pain, and offered Jack his hand. "C'mon, let me buy you a beer while I can still afford it."

Jack took his hand, Jesse pulled him to his feet and together they straggled silently towards the restaurant, carrying their packages.

★ ★ ★

Mark came home exhausted, expecting to find the house ransacked, but was stunned to discover that everything was very neat and tidy. He supposed he had Tanis to thank for that. Any other cop probably would have left the place looking like a particularly vindictive tornado had passed through it.

For once, Steve had beaten him home and had already changed into jeans and a T-shirt. He was standing on the deck, his back to Mark, drinking a beer and watching the sun set over the Pacific. Mark joined him at the railing and felt a refreshing chill in the air. He was grateful for it. On the other side of the Santa Monica Mountains behind them, in the smog-choked flatlands of the San Fernando Valley, it was probably eighty-five degrees and muggy.

Steve glanced at his Dad and grinned to himself. "You look terrible."

"I've had kind of a long day," Mark said.

"So I've heard," Steve replied. "While I was out in the valley, trying to quietly check up on Lydia Yates without showing up on the chief's radar, I understand you were in his office accusing him of putting politics before justice."

"You think that might have alerted him to what you were doing?" asked Mark facetiously, knowing that the chief had all but promised Mark that Steve would pay for his father's actions.

"Yeah," Steve said, "I think it might have."

"What sort of indications did you get?"

"The first indication I had was when he suspended me with pay pending an internal affairs investigation. The second indication I had was when I was leaving the building and bumped into a couple uniforms who gave me a hard time about my Neil Diamond collection," Steve looked hard at his father. "Nobody knows about my Neil Diamond collection."

"*I* didn't know about your Neil Diamond collection," Mark said.

"That's because it's hidden. So I deduced that the officers must have been in our house searching for something, and searching hard," Steve said. "For that, they must have had a warrant, which was my third indication that the chief was alerted to what I was doing."

Steve was grinning and showing no real anger, but Mark knew he'd put his son's career at risk.

Mark dropped the light pretense and put

his arm around his son. "I'm sorry, Steve. I put my own interests before yours. It was wrong."

"You were right to do what you did. It took guts to stand up to the chief, more than most men would have," Steve said. "I'm proud of you."

Mark gave his son's shoulder a squeeze and sighed with relief. "I just get carried away sometimes."

"Yeah, but this time it's for the right reasons. If we do nothing about it and this psychopath kills someone else, we're going to feel like accomplices. I don't know about you, but that's something I'd like to avoid."

"How do you know I'm right?"

"I'm trusting your stats," Steve said. "Eight out of ten times you're right."

"Nine out of ten," Mark said.

"I don't think so."

"Just so happens I visited a UCLA professor of mathematics and had him calculate the figures for me," Mark said.

"So I heard."

Mark filled Steve in on the suspicious circumstances surrounding Stanley Tidewell's death and his belief that it was murder. Ordinarily, Steve would have jumped right on it, but considering that he'd just been suspended, and that Mark wasn't exactly welcome downtown right now, Steve thought it might make more sense for them to investigate independently and build a stronger case to eventually bring to the police. Mark thought that was sound advice.

The subject of independent investigation brought Mark back to his ongoing inquiry into old serial killings.

"Did you come up with anything on Lydia Yates before I got you suspended?" Mark asked.

"I talked to enough people to know she didn't have a single enemy," Steve said. "I think she was a random target in the wrong place at the wrong time."

"So do I." Mark went on to explain his discovery of the Oakes Root Beer bottle cap at three of the murder scenes and why he believed this proved another killer was at work.

"I'd like to go through the case files you didn't get to last night," Steve said. "I'll see if I can find any more murders where that bottle cap shows up in the evidence gathered at the scene."

"You don't have to do this."

"You get some rest, Dad. You need it. It's my turn to stay up all night."

"You're going to need some help," Mark said.

"I've got plenty," Steve said, tilting his head towards the kitchen.

Mark turned and was astonished, and more than a little touched, to see Amanda and Tanis coming outside, each of them holding a beer. He knew he could always depend on Amanda, but the fact that Tanis was putting herself on the line for him was a genuine surprise.

Amanda smiled slyly at Steve.

"How come you don't bring me flowers any more?" she asked in a singsong voice.

"Don't you start," Steve warned her.

"I bet if we looked harder," Tanis said to Amanda, "we'd have found a John Denver collection, too." Tanis shifted her attention to Mark. "But I'm sure we never would have found those serial killer case files, even if we stripped this house down to the studs."

Mark just smiled enigmatically. "I've lost quite a few socks over the years; you didn't happen to find any of them, did you?"

"The chief was furious," Tanis continued. "He's having warrants drawn up to search your office at Community General."

"If his officers clean up my office the way they did my house, he'll be doing me a big favor," Mark said. "You're risking a lot by being here."

Tanis shrugged. "Depends on how you define a lot. Can't go much further down than the subbasement of Parker Center."

"You sure the LAPD doesn't have some kind of sewer patrol?" Amanda asked.

"I may find out," Tanis said.

"I didn't think I'd convinced you that Lydia Yates was killed by someone else," Mark said.

"You didn't," Tanis said. "But *you're* convinced, and that's enough for me." She smiled conspiratorially at him. "So, c'mon, you can tell me now. Where did you hide the files?"

Mark glanced at Steve and could see from the look on his face that his son had already figured it out.

"Ask Steve," Mark said, and went inside.

The two women looked at Steve. He just smiled and nodded towards the beach. "Don't you think my dad is a little old to be making sand castles?"

Tanis and Amanda joined Steve at the wooden railing and looked over the side. On the beach below were three lopsided sandcastles, the kind a child might make by filling a plastic bucket with hard-packed sand and then turning it over. Tanis felt incredibly stupid. How could she have missed that?

"He buried the files," Tanis said, "and left the castles so he'd remember where."

"There are some advantages to having nothing but sand for a backyard," Steve said. "For one thing, you can bury stuff without disturbing the surface and drawing any attention."

"Hey," Amanda said to Steve, "I think we just found the perfect spot for your Neil Diamond collection."

CHAPTER THIRTEEN

Jesse and Jack sat across from each other in a booth in the back of BBQ Bob's. They both held dishrags filled with ice against their swollen faces. The remains of two rib dinners and several beers filled the table between them.

"I've got to ask you a question," Jesse said. "Just between you and me, why did you go off to Colorado?"

"It wasn't the money, and it wasn't really the medical challenge, either. It was the life they were offering me. They flew me out there, and it was beautiful. Clean air, blue skies, actual seasons. I saw the trees, the skiing and the women," Jack said. "Especially the women. Do you know what they wear under those skintight ski suits? Nothing. Absolutely nothing."

Jesse whistled slowly. "Wow."

"Look, I loved working at the hospital with Mark and Amanda, and helping Mark with his investigations was interesting and exciting, but I missed having some free time; I missed having some fun," Jack said. "Have you ever gone out partying with Steve Sloan?"

"Hell, no."

"Then you know exactly what I mean," Jack said. "He's like a babe repellent."

They shared a laugh together, until a cut on Jesse's lip broke open again and he started to bleed.

"As long as we're being honest, I've got something to admit," Jesse said, dabbing his lip with a napkin. "There's a reason I've been such a jerk to you. The truth is, it took me years to stop feeling like your stand-in. I knew that everything I did would be compared to you and that I'd fall short."

"Not any more. We're equally negligent and incompetent, at least to Billy Tidewell," Jack said, paging through the lawsuit with one hand. "You should be thrilled."

"I was talking about Mark."

"Mark isn't like that," Jack replied, pushing the lawsuit aside. "You have his respect the moment he meets you, and it takes a lot to lose it. Believe me, I know."

"He's proud of you, Jack. That's obvious."

"He was," Jack said. "But then I let him

down by leaving. Didn't take him very long to find someone to take my place." He glanced at Jesse. "Proves I wasn't so special after all. That's why I had to make you look stupid thirty seconds after I got here, to show he was wrong."

Jesse eyed Jack skeptically. "You know yourself that well?"

"Of course not. I'm a guy, I don't have a clue why I do what I do," Jack said. "I'm just repeating what Amanda said while she was screaming at me about the way I treated you."

"Amanda did that?" Jesse picked a tiny piece of broken glass out of his hair and set it with the tiny smattering of other shards he'd collected on his manila envelope.

"She loves to scream at me," Jack said.

Jesse grinned, then abruptly stopped because it irritated his split lip. "She likes to scream at me, too. Though, to be honest, I irritate her a lot on purpose."

Jack played intently with a French fry on his plate for a moment. Jesse didn't say anything, just listened to the reassuring din of customers talking, utensils clattering against dishes and the rock-and-roll classics coming from the jukebox.

"So, what's the deal with you and Susan?" Jack asked.

"Why?" Jesse asked, narrowing his one unswollen eye. "Are you interested in her?"

"No, no, no," Jack said, raising his free hand to stop that thought, and perhaps another punch, in its tracks. "You don't have to worry about that. I just noticed you two really seem to have something special going. It's obvious that she really cares about you."

"We've been together for a few years now, and between you and me" — Jesse leaned towards Jack across the table, and lowered his voice — "I've been working up the guts to propose to her."

"For how long?" Jack asked, lowering his voice to a near whisper.

"A few years now."

They both sat up and laughed, even though it hurt in a dozen places.

"Hey, man," Jack said, "I'm sorry about kicking your ass."

"That's the second time you've apologized to me," Jesse said. "I think it's my turn now. Besides, I kicked *your* ass."

"Tell you what," Jack said, setting his icepack on the table. "Help me find whoever killed Stanley Tidewell and we'll call it even."

Jesse touched his lip again, then checked his finger to see if it came away bloody. It still did. "I don't blame you for coming after me. I would have come after me myself if I were you. But if you're willing to scratch me off your list of suspects, I've got a pretty good idea who to start with."

"Who?"

"You remember a nurse named Teresa Chingas?" Jesse asked.

"No," Jack replied.

"Okay," Jesse said. "You just validated her motive right there."

"I did?" Jack asked, lost.

"We'll come back to that," Jesse said. "Let's go over the people on both surgical teams and see who else might have a grudge against you or Stanley Tidewell."

Jesse reached for a fresh napkin, pulled a ballpoint pen from his shirt pocket and got ready to write.

Mark slept until nine thirty the next morning, paying off a sleep debt going back a few days. A fog bank had rolled in during the night and there was a chill in the air. He got into his sweats and padded barefoot out of the bedroom to get a little breakfast.

As he came down the hall, he felt the buzz of activity before he was actually aware of the many new voices, the hum of fax machines, the sounds of people in motion.

He stepped into the living room and was astounded to see it had been converted into a bustling office manned by Steve, Amanda, Tanis, and two men wearing bright blue windbreakers with "FBI" stenciled in big white letters on the back. His furniture had been jammed into the kitchen and replaced with folding chairs and long tables that were covered with laptop computers, fax machines, stacks of files and even various copies of Freddy Meeks' true crime books. A huge bulletin board had been hung above his fireplace and was already plastered with crime scene photos and maps of California and Los Angeles, both dotted with pins that, Mark presumed, represented murder victims. There were five pins now. Two more victims had been discovered while he slept. Apparently, he'd slept through a lot.

Steve was the first to notice Mark standing there, his mouth agape. "Morning, Dad."

"I must be one heavy sleeper," Mark said. "What's going on here?"

Steve pulled Mark aside. "The investigation has expanded a bit over the last few hours."

"So I see," Mark said, watching one of the FBI agents pour sand from a file into a garbage can.

"Last night we found two more murders with our guy's calling card, the Oakes Diet Root Beer bottle cap, at the scene of the crime," Steve said. "I'm afraid there could be even more killings he's responsible for, but the three of us have gone as far as we can go with the files you buried. We needed more information, but we couldn't go back to the LAPD to ask for it, could we?"

"So you called in the FBI," Mark said.

"They were willing to help," Steve said, a little defensively.

"I'm sure they were," Mark said. The fact that the LAPD and FBI didn't cooperate with one another was hardly a secret. The dispute amounted to a jurisdictional cold war that had existed for decades. There was only one reason they'd overlook the ingrained, institutional animosity to help his son. The FBI saw a chance to embarrass the LAPD.

"This was too good an opportunity for them to pass up," Mark said. "They're taking advantage of us on the chance they can score a victory against the LAPD."

"It's not like that, Dad. Over the years,

I've developed a back-channel relationship with an agent there," Steve said. "We both feel it's in our best interests to quietly share information on key cases despite the jurisdictional rivalry. So, when I realized we had nowhere else to go, I woke him up at three this morning and told him all about what you'd discovered."

"And he was convinced right away?" Mark asked, dubious.

"He was here within the hour," Steve said. "He's promising to put the full resources of the bureau behind this."

A third FBI agent in a windbreaker brushed past them, wheeling in more boxes on a hand truck. These boxes were marked with the FBI insignia. Mark led Steve further aside, out of earshot of the others.

"The only reason they jumped into this, no questions asked, is because they risk nothing if I'm wrong and have everything to gain if I'm right," Mark said, speaking in a low voice. "They would love the chance to expose the fact that the LAPD bungled several high-profile serial-killer cases and, in doing so, let another murderer go on killing undetected for a decade."

"It's the truth," Steve said.

"But the FBI will come out of this the

heroes, and the LAPD will suffer another humiliating blow," Mark said. "You will be blamed for it. You will be vilified as a traitor."

"If that's what it costs to stop this killer from taking another life, then so be it," Steve said. "It's a price I'm willing to pay."

"And if I'm wrong, and there isn't another serial killer, you've just committed career suicide," Mark said. "You'll never work in law enforcement again in any capacity anywhere in this country."

"You mean I might have to move back home and live with my parents?" Steve said with a grin. "I'm already one step ahead of the game."

But Mark wasn't amused. "You know what I'm saying, Steve."

"Look, you aren't wrong, Dad. There *is* another serial killer out there. And if I wasn't a cop, you wouldn't be worried about embarrassing the LAPD. You'd have gone straight to the FBI yourself the instant Chief Masters threw you out of his office. So forget about my career; it doesn't matter. Catching this killer does."

Mark always knew his son Steve was a good cop, but he'd never seen a better example of his courage and integrity. He was so proud of his son, he didn't know what to say. Instead, he just gave him a warm hug. The sudden show of affection caught Steve by surprise, which quickly turned to embarrassment when he saw the others watching. Steve gently pulled away.

"It's not just me, you know," Steve said. "I discussed this with Amanda and Tanis first. They agreed that we should take this to the Feds."

"I'll hug them later," Mark said jokingly, knowing how uncomfortable Steve had always been with any kind of affection.

Steve waved over one of the FBI agents who'd been watching them both out of the corner of his eye as he worked. "Dad, let me introduce you to Special Agent Terry Riordan."

Terry strode over and gave Mark a firm handshake. He was a big Texan with a grip that could pulverize bone. "It's an honor to meet you, Dr. Sloan. I've followed your accomplishments in homicide investigation for many years. You did the right thing bringing us in on the Silent Partner investigation."

"The Silent Partner?" Mark asked, massaging his sore hand.

"The serial killer who's hidden his kills on the scorecards of other psychopaths, like he was their silent partner in crime,"

Terry said. "We like to give our targets names. Helps us focus."

"I see," Mark replied.

"Besides, we like to beat the tabloids to it," Terry said. "Their names are always a little too lurid for our taste, but they stick."

"Why are you setting up your operation here?" Mark asked, motioning to all the activity. "Why aren't you running the investigation out of the Federal Building?"

"To be honest, I'm afraid that Masters has eyes and ears in the building and that he'll find out quickly what we're doing if we set up a task force there," Terry said. "I think we can accomplish more if we don't get bogged down at the outset in political infighting and jurisdictional disputes with the LAPD. So we're keeping this low-key."

"Which is why you're wearing your FBI windbreakers on the street and wheeling boxes with the FBI insignia into my house," Mark said.

Terry looked down at his jacket as if noticing it for the first time, then shrugged self-consciously. "It was chilly this morning."

"Well, make yourself at home," Mark said, suddenly feeling in desperate need of a hot shower and plenty of caffeine. "Let me know how I can help."

"It's the other way around, Dr. Sloan," Terry said. "This is your investigation; you're the point man on this task force."

Mark regarded the agent skeptically. "No offense, Agent Riordan, but that doesn't sound very FBI-like to me."

"This hasn't been designated an official investigation, if you know what I mean," Terry said. "This is sort of an off-the-books operation at the moment, something we're doing strictly for the good of the community."

"Until it's time to make an arrest," Mark said. "Then I suspect it will suddenly become a full-blown, official FBI investigation."

"We won't forget to give credit where credit is due," Terry said, glancing at Steve.

"Or apportion blame," Mark said.

"That will be up to the public to decide," Terry said, meeting Mark's gaze. "If there's a problem here, we can pack up and go, pretend this never happened."

Mark knew that was an empty offer. The FBI would continue to pursue the investigation with or without him now. It was too good an opportunity to take a shot at the LAPD. Besides, Steve brought the FBI into this with his eyes open; it benefited no one to turn away their cooperation now. Mark simply wanted the bureau's motivations out in the open, so everyone knew where everybody stood.

"Not at all, Agent Riordan. I'm grateful you're here," Mark said. "You'll have to forgive me; I'm always irritable until I've had my morning coffee."

"I'm the same way, Dr. Sloan. And please, call me Terry. We'll keep you informed the moment we come up with anything." And with that, Terry returned to the living room, peeling off his windbreaker on the way.

Mark turned to his son. "You know Masters will find out about this by the end of the day."

Steve nodded in agreement. "If he doesn't know already. There's not much he can do to stop us now without risking making our investigation public. He can't let that happen."

"Not with five victims and counting," Mark said, glancing at the bulletin board above his fireplace.

"We're broadening our scope, now that the FBI is involved," Steve said. "We're looking at every serial-killer case in the western United States going back ten years. We need to see just how long the Silent Partner has been at this and how far he's traveled."

Mark gave him a look. " 'The Silent Partner'?"

Steve shrugged. "Giving the guy a name helps me focus, too."

Mark glanced at his watch. "I've got to go to the hospital and start looking into what happened to Stanley Tidewell. I'll check back with you this afternoon."

"Yeah, keep me informed on this Tidewell thing, too. Is there any evidence of murder besides the test results from Amanda's autopsy?"

"No," Mark said. "And there isn't going to be."

"Why not?" Steve asked.

"Immediately after the operation all the instruments went to central supply for resterilization and all the disposable items were tossed away as infectious waste," Mark said. "It's standard procedure. The murderer was very clever. He or she knew whatever evidence there was would get thrown away."

"So we've got nothing to go on."

"Not exactly," Mark said. "We have the corpse."

CHAPTER FOURTEEN

That morning, Mike and Ken were broadcasting live from the public restroom on Venice Beach. Since Mike and Ken seemed to be clairvoyant, Mark tuned in on his way to Community General, hoping to learn who killed Stanley Tidewell, who the Silent Partner was and whether Chief Masters knew Steve had invited the FBI into the investigation.

Instead, Mark got to hear their special guest Herb Schlott, an avid Trekker, flatulate the *Star Trek* theme while Ken accompanied him with an imitation of William Shatner's voice-over.

Mike and Ken might have revealed the news Mark was waiting for later, but he would never know. He turned the radio off well before Herb finished his solo performance.

Mark didn't know which was more upsetting, that this repulsive garbage was on the air, or that Steve and Jesse enjoyed listening to it.

He traveled the rest of the way to the hospital in silence, alone with his thoughts. There was a lot to think about. There was the unsettling reality that a serial killer was on the loose in L.A. and had been killing with impunity for years. And if Mark didn't stop him, more people would die and his son's career would be destroyed.

As if that wasn't enough weighing on his mind, he also had to deal with the disturbing revelation that one of his patients was murdered at his hospital, probably by a member of his medical staff. And if Mark couldn't expose the killer, Jack's future as a doctor could be ruined.

Even if Mark could catch the serial killer and whoever killed Stanley Tidewell, the reputations of two institutions he cared deeply about, the Los Angeles Police Department and Community General Hospital, would almost certainly be irreparably tarnished.

The pressure he felt was enormous. Mark tried to relax and clear his head. He knew himself well enough to know he did his best thinking by not actively thinking at all, letting his subconscious do the heavy lifting. So he concentrated instead on the beautiful morning.

The top was down on his Saab convertible, and he enjoyed the cool morning air. The scent of the ocean slowly dissipated the closer he got to the hospital. He noticed, as he always did, how the outdoor temperature gauge on his dashboard rapidly ticked up by five degrees. If he were to keep heading east, then cut north into the valley, he'd see the temperature jump another ten degrees, and the vestiges of the ocean spray in the air would be smothered by the acrid stench of car exhaust. Smog lingered in the valley, trapped in the bowl formed by the mountains around it, hanging like a brown tarp over the flatlands until the Santa Ana winds blew it free or rain washed it down onto the streets.

He drove into the five-story Community General parking structure and wound his way up to the third floor, where he had his coveted assigned parking spot across from the sky-bridge to the hospital.

As Mark parked in his spot, he noticed the souped-up Honda Accord coupe that was backed into Dr. Smollen's space at the top of the aisle, just before the turn to the upper level. The car had tinted windows and racing stripes, and its motor was running. The passenger side was facing Mark, the dark window rolled down just a crack.

Mark knew it wasn't Dr. Smollen, since the doctor drove a Cadillac and had a virulent hatred of Japanese cars. Dr. Smollen often made the tired xenophobic observation that the Japanese might have lost World War II, but they had conquered our economy instead, invading us with their cheap and dependable cars, then using their ill-gotten gains to buy our land and our corporations. Dr. Smollen didn't seem to dislike Japanese individuals, at least not that Mark had noticed, but he had a healthy dislike of the country, the government and their automakers.

So, whoever was in Dr. Smollen's space in a Japanese car had definitely not been invited to park there. Which was why as Mark emerged from his car and started towards the sky-bridge across from him, he couldn't help slowing his pace to see what Dr. Smollen, who was driving up from the lower level now, would do when he saw the car in his spot.

The Honda edged out as Mark stepped into the center of the lane, the passenger window rolling down. Mark couldn't see the driver, but he saw the gun. His heart skipped a beat in terror.

Without even thinking, Mark kicked off and rolled on his wheeled sneakers just as the first shot rang out, the bullet shattering the rear window of the parked car across from him. The gunshot echoed in the parking structure like an explosion, making his ears ring. Mark skated towards the safety of the crowded sky-bridge, then realized he'd be putting the people on it in deadly jeopardy, so he sped down the ramp instead, bent over aerodynamically like a downhill skier.

The Honda sped out of the parking spot, screeched into a turn and raced down the lane after him. On his wheeled sneakers, heading down the steep ramp, Mark was picking up speed with every second and becoming more terrified. The faster he went, the greater the chances he'd lose control, take a tumble and look up just in time to see the tread of the tires that would grind him into the asphalt. But he had bigger worries.

Mark was heading straight for Dr. Smollen's Cadillac, putting his friend in danger of either colliding with the gunman's car or catching an errant bullet meant for Mark. So Mark abruptly turned to his right, cutting between two parked cars and flying onto the lower level below, nearly losing his balance but gaining a vital head start on his pursuer.

The speeding Honda sideswiped Dr. Smollen's Cadillac, shearing off the mirror and scraping the entire length of his car in a hail of sparks. The gunman's car fishtailed around the turn in a scream of burning rubber and tore down the ramp after Mark. The driver aimed his gun out the driver's side window, firing off shots.

Mark weaved to make himself less of a target as bullets ricocheted off the asphalt and pinged into cars all around him. He didn't know what to do. He might be able to dodge the bullets for a while, but he couldn't outrace a car. In a few seconds, the car would mow him down. He'd never been more scared in his life.

Ahead of him, Mark could see the elevator and the stairs. If he could get to the stairwell, he'd be safe. He was about to put everything he had into reaching the stairs, when he saw two nurses emerge from the elevator. If he went there, any bullet that missed him could hit one of them.

It was a risk he couldn't take.

Mark whizzed around the next turn. A Lexus suddenly pulled out of a parking spot in front of him. Mark abruptly weaved around behind it, barely avoiding being crushed between the rear of the Lexus and a parked car. He wobbled, barely maintaining control, and raced on, the friction under his sneakers generating so much heat it felt like his feet were on fire.

The Lexus blocked the path of the oncoming Honda, which slammed into it like a bumper car, knocking it out of the way. The gunman grazed a row of parked cars, shaving off bumpers and smashing taillights, then bore down on Mark.

But Mark was already making the next, and final, turn, heading down the ramp towards the ticket booth, the yellow-and-black-striped gate arm and the cross-traffic on the busy street beyond it.

There was another deafening gunshot and Mark saw the glass of the ticket booth explode, the attendant diving under his desk for cover. Mark ducked below the gate arm, passing safely under it, and burst out of the parking structure into the traffic.

Cars screeched to a stop, swerved and jumped the curb to avoid hitting Mark as he blasted past them, heading towards the alley on the other side of the street. An instant later the mangled Honda, dragging its bumper, flew out of the parking structure after him and careened into the street, clipping a stalled car and sending it spinning.

Mark shot up a loading ramp and flew

headfirst into a metal trash Dumpster, landing hard in a pile of cardboard boxes, plastic wrap and Styrofoam packing material. The wrecked Honda charged into the alley, scraping the Dumpsters and the narrow walls on either side before speeding into the street on the other end, fishtailing into traffic and driving off.

Mark remained still in the Dumpster, dazed and winded, dimly aware of the blood trickling down his forehead, his feet throbbing and the sound of sirens closing in the distance.

An hour later, crime scene techs were crawling all over the Community General Hospital parking structure and the length of the alley across the street, snapping pictures, measuring skid marks and prying bullets out of cement, tires and bucket seats. Uniformed officers were taking statements from shaken witnesses. Doctors from the hospital were in the street, treating the minor cuts and scrapes suffered by drivers in the various car accidents sparked by the attempt on Mark Sloan's life. And TV reporters from the news-starved local stations were carefully positioning themselves so their cameras could catch all the activity behind them during their live broadcasts from the scene.

Steve strode up to Lt. Sam Rykus, a stout, bored, perpetually weary detective who always seemed to be chewing on a fat cigar. Rykus was standing outside the alley, gazing at the destruction with the calm detachment of a guy watching ducks in a pond.

"I figured you'd be turning up sooner or later," Rykus said.

"Someone shot at my father," Steve said. "I'd be here whether I had a badge or not."

"You don't," Rykus said casually. "At least, that's the scuttlebutt."

Steve shrugged. "The chief and I are having creative differences."

Rykus chewed on his cigar. "Your dad always run around with skates on?"

"It's one of his eccentricities," Steve said, rubbing his eyes. It had been a long night and it was shaping up to be an even longer day. "I can give you a list of his others, if you like."

"I'd prefer a list of possible suspects," Rykus said. "Your father wasn't very forthcoming about who was shooting at him."

"Probably because my father doesn't know," Steve said.

"Do you?" Rykus asked.

"My father has helped put a lot of people in prison," Steve said. "If I were you, I'd check to see if any of them have been paroled recently. I'd also check if anybody he put away has been hurt or killed behind bars. That might have given somebody a reason to come gunning for Dad now."

"What's your dad been working on lately?" Rykus asked.

"The chief's Blue Ribbon Task Force on Unsolved Homicides," Steve replied. "Or at least he was until yesterday afternoon."

"Nothing else?" Rykus asked.

Steve thought about mentioning Stanley Tidewell's death, but it was too early to call it murder, at least officially, nor had his dad actually started investigating yet. So Steve just shook his head no.

"You got anything to go on?" Steve asked.

"We got a solid description of the car and a partial plate," Rykus said, "but I'm sure the car is gonna turn out to be stolen."

Steve nodded. He was sure, too. "Anybody see the driver?"

"Any witnesses who weren't diving for cover had air bags blowing up in their faces," Rykus said. "Nobody saw the driver; all they saw was a gun. Besides, the car had tinted windows."

"What about the bullets?"

"We've recovered some shells," Rykus said. "They're on the way to the lab."

Steve looked at the wrecked cars, the broken glass, the skid marks in the street and the dented Dumpster in the alley that had saved his father's life.

"Was anybody seriously hurt?" Steve asked.

Rykus shook his head. "Just the insurance companies. Has anybody ever suggested to your dad that he stick to medicine?"

Steve motioned to the street. "I think somebody just did."

CHAPTER FIFTEEN

Mark was behind a curtain in the E.R., sitting on a gurney and wincing as Jesse stitched up the nasty cut on his forehead. He didn't enjoy being a patient, though it was better than being a corpse.

"It's amazing you're alive. You should be a bullet-riddled corpse with a tire tread across your chest," Jesse said. "But I hear you rode those Heelys of yours like a champion roller skater. Dodging hot lead. Rolling into speeding traffic. Flying headfirst into a metal Dumpster. You're lucky you walked away from this with only some cuts and bruises."

"So, how come you look worse than I do?" Mark asked.

"We can talk about that later," Jesse said. "Any idea who wanted to kill you?"

"I like to think of myself as a nice guy, but the fact is, I've made quite a few enemies over the years," Mark said. "It could be any of them. Any idea who tried to kill *you?*"

As if on cue, the curtain opened and Jack came in, with a face to match Jesse's. Mark immediately realized what had happened and then felt foolish that he hadn't seen it coming. But he'd been too distracted by his serial-killer investigation to see the obvious signs of growing discord between Jack and Jesse. It made Mark wonder what else he'd missed over the last few days and if it might lead to whoever tried to kill him this morning.

"How are you feeling?" Jack asked.

"From the look of things, about the same as you," Mark said to Jack. "You actually thought Jesse tainted Stanley's kidney with penicillin?"

"No," Jack said. "Why would you say that?"

"Let's just say I read it on your face." Mark then glanced at Jesse. "And yours."

"There was a bar fight at BBQ Bob's last night," Jesse said. "Jack jumped right into the middle of it and tried to help me out."

"Really?" Mark knew Jesse was lying but was pleased he was trying. It meant that Jack and Jesse had resolved their differences and were friends now. Only friends looked out for each other with lies like that.

"I went down to talk to him about the lawsuit," Jack said.

"What lawsuit?" Mark asked.

"We're being sued for thirty million dollars by Stanley Tidewell's son for wrongful death and medical malpractice," Jack said. "So's the hospital."

Mark now had thirty million more reasons to focus his attention on Stanley's death. He slid off the gurney and faced Jack. "I want you to put together a list of both surgical teams involved in the transplant and tell me if you know anyone who might have a reason to hurt you or kill Stanley Tidewell."

"I don't know about Stanley," Jack said, "but Jesse and I have put together a list of people in the O.R. who might have had a grudge against me."

Jesse handed Mark a napkin with several names written on it. "The only person I know of in the O.R. with a motive to kill Stanley was me. Stanley was going to build a Burger Beach outlet across the street from BBQ Bob's."

"I didn't know that," Mark said, pocketing the napkin.

"Steve did," Jesse replied. "So did Amanda."

Mark was surprised no one had told

him. Then again, maybe they had. He'd been distracted.

"But killing Stanley would be no guarantee that his son or the company wouldn't go ahead and build the restaurant anyway," Mark said.

"Yeah, but killing him would sure make me feel better," Jesse said, "assuming I was the vengeful, homicidal type."

"There is that," Mark agreed.

With Jack essentially cleared of negligence, Mark had to admit that Jesse now became the most logical suspect. If Burger Beach drove BBQ Bob's out of business, Jesse would be drowning in debt. Come to think of it, Mark thought, so would Steve, and by extension, himself. As an investor in BBQ Bob's, he also had good reason to be murderously angry with Stanley Tidewell.

Mark knew it wouldn't take long for Billy Tidewell's lawyers to come to the same conclusion and use the circumstantial evidence to convince the jury there was a homicidal conspiracy behind Stanley's death. Suddenly, the civil case against Community General Hospital was looking a lot stronger.

The curtain opened and Steve came in. He stopped and stared at the three bruised and bandaged doctors with a puzzled expression on his face.

"Don't ask," Mark said. "But since you're here, I think we should talk to everyone involved in Stanley Tidewell's surgery."

"You think that might have something to do with the attempt on your life?" Steve asked.

Mark shook his head. "The official line is that Stanley died because of an allergic reaction to an antibiotic that Jack gave him. No one knows yet that we suspect it was murder. Of course, that will change after we start asking questions."

"What do you want us to do?" Jack asked.

"Nothing for now," Mark replied. "We'll contact you both as soon as we have something to go on."

Mark walked out into the hall with Steve, who noticed his father was a little unsteady on his feet.

"Are you sure you're okay?" Steve asked, taking his father's arm.

"I'm fine," Mark said. "It's my shoes that need help."

Mark leaned on his son, took off his sneakers and showed him the soles. The rubber treads looked as if they'd been sanded nearly smooth, and the tiny wheel in the heel was lopsided, chipped and cracked.

"I won't be getting much more use out of these," Mark said, and was about to drop them in a nearby trash can when Steve stopped him.

"No way," Steve said, taking the shoes with a grin. "We're putting these on display."

So far that day, Nurse Teresa Chingas had been puked on twice and sprayed with blood once, and she had seen two patients expertly cracked open by blasé surgeons.

Teresa had gotten past being bothered or sickened by people vomiting, bleeding or losing control of their bladders or bowels on her. She knew they didn't mean to do it, and she was acutely aware of their embarrassment and shame.

What she'd been unable to get used to was the intimacy of looking inside a person's body, of seeing their internal organs exposed to the light, of seeing them far more naked than they ever thought they could be. There was something deeply unsettling about it, a feeling that she was violating them, even though she knew she was helping to save their lives.

One of the ways she dealt with that discomfort was to take her breaks far from the chaos of the E.R. She'd buy a coke and a bag of chips from the vending machines, scrounge up a discarded magazine or newspaper, then find a room upstairs with an empty bed. Teresa would close the door, drag the guest chair to the window and enjoy the solitude.

Which was exactly what she was doing when Mark Sloan, the chief of internal medicine, came into the room in his stocking feet, startling her. She stood up quickly, certain that she was about to be reprimanded. Teresa wasn't entirely sure that what she'd been doing for so many years was against the rules, though it always had a strangely forbidden feeling to it.

"Excuse me, Teresa, I didn't mean to startle you," Mark said amiably. "The nurses told me I might find you here. Please sit down. I'd like to talk with you for a few minutes."

That's when Teresa noticed Mark wasn't alone. There was a stranger with him.

"Of course," she replied, sitting down slowly in her seat. If she wasn't going to be chastised for occupying a vacant patient room, what could this be about?

"Teresa, this is my son Steve," Mark

said, sitting on the edge of the bed. "He's with the LAPD."

Steve flashed his badge and remained standing. Teresa shifted uneasily in her seat. No one was ever comfortable with the police, he thought, even if they'd never done anything wrong. Of course, it didn't help that he was intentionally standing over her, looking down at her with a stone face.

"We have a few questions about Stanley Tidewell's death," Mark said.

"Isn't this something for the review committee?" she asked. "Why are the police involved?"

"Because Stanley Tidewell was murdered," Mark replied.

"I thought he died from an allergic reaction to an antibiotic," she said. "That it was an accident."

"Actually, he was poisoned," Mark said. "Stanley was allergic to penicillin. During the operation, someone tainted his new kidney with it. It couldn't have been an accident."

"You think it was me?" Teresa asked disbelievingly.

"We're just exploring all the possibilities," Mark said.

"I didn't do it," she said.

"You were the one who carried the organ from one operating room to the other," Steve said. "What else are we supposed to think?"

"I've never even met Stanley Tidewell," she said. "I had no reason to hurt him."

"But you'd met Jack Stewart," Steve said. "Intimately. You were lovers before he left here, but when he showed up at Community General again, he didn't even recognize you. That must have done wonders for your self-esteem."

"You think I intentionally botched the operation to get back at him?"

"I'm afraid it looks that way," Mark said sympathetically. "You had motive and, frankly, the best opportunity of anyone to sabotage the kidney. A death during a transplant operation could have ruined Jack's reputation as a surgeon. It might even have cost him his medical license."

"He won't forget you now, will he?" Steve said.

"If I wanted to ruin Jack, I could have done it a long time ago," she said softly.

Teresa looked from one Sloan to the other and took a deep breath, resigning herself to what she had to say.

"Before Jack left, I found out I was pregnant."

Mark shared a surprised look with Steve, who in turn regarded Teresa with open skepticism.

"You can check my medical records if you want," she said, "though I don't suppose I can prove he was the father now."

"Did Jack know you were pregnant?" Mark asked.

She shook her head. "If I'd told him, he would never have left L.A. Jack would have refused the job in Denver, and all the opportunities it offered him, to stay here with me."

"How do you know he would have done that?" Steve asked.

"Because Jack would have been terrified of losing your respect," Teresa said, looking at Mark. "If he left me behind with his child, he knew what you'd think about him. What you thought of him, Dr. Sloan, was more important to Jack than anything. I knew that, and I could have used it against him, but I didn't. I let him go."

"What happened to the baby?" Mark asked.

"I miscarried." She swallowed hard. It still surprised her how fresh the pain was, even after all these years.

"Sounds to me like you have an even better motive than we thought," Steve said.

Teresa glared at him, her pain and discomfort turning very quickly to anger.

"I haven't told Jack about the pregnancy or the miscarriage," she said. "If I wanted to hurt him, *that's* how I would do it, not by killing a patient. Look, maybe I did poison the kidney. Anybody could have laced the saline with penicillin before I added it to the organ pan. I wouldn't have known."

She has a point, Mark thought to himself.

"But nobody had your motive," Steve said.

Except for Jesse, Mark thought.

Perhaps Mark's misgivings showed on his face, because Teresa focused her attention on him, purposely ignoring the big, mean, insensitive cop standing over her.

"I knew that Jack didn't love me, and that the baby wouldn't change that," she said. "I didn't resent him for it; in fact, I sympathized with him."

Steve shook his head. "You've lost me."

"Jack was feeling the same agony I was, the pain of realizing you love someone who is never going to want you," Teresa said. "Why do you think Jack left Community General? It hurt too much to be near her."

"Who was it?" Mark asked.

"I was hoping you could tell me," she said, a touch of sadness in her voice.

CHAPTER SIXTEEN

Mark and Steve questioned all the members of both surgical teams. Teresa wasn't the only nurse Jack had slept with, but the others didn't harbor any ill feelings towards him. The same couldn't be said of Billy Tidewell's anesthesiologist, Dwight Tatum. It seemed that Jack had accused Tatum eight years ago of negligence involving a patient. The complaint was investigated and dismissed by the hospital's review committee, but the accusation had hung over Tatum for some time anyway.

There were at least three people that Mark knew of involved in the operation with motives to ruin Jack Stewart, and one of them was Jesse. Mark didn't know yet if anyone on the surgical teams besides Jesse had anything against Stanley Tidewell.

But as Nurse Teresa Chingas had pointed out, anyone could have spiked the saline solution with penicillin before the operation took place.

And that's exactly what Mark explained

to Jack, Jesse and Amanda when they all gathered in the pathology lab that afternoon to compare notes. There were some facts Mark didn't reveal to them. He didn't think it was necessary to tell Jack about Teresa's pregnancy and subsequent miscarriage. That was Teresa's decision to make.

"So where does this leave us?" Jesse asked, after digesting everything Mark had to say.

Mark sighed. "We aren't going to solve the mystery by interrogating the medical staff. I think our best hope is to re-create both operations. Maybe if I see what each person was doing, and when they were doing it, I might get a better sense of how the murderer got away with it. Then, maybe, we can work backwards to establish a motive."

Mark turned to Amanda, who looked tired after her long night going through the FBI files. "Can you get us two cadavers we can use? I want this re-creation to be as authentic as possible."

"Sure," Amanda said.

Steve came in, a strange expression on his face.

"What is it?" Mark asked, concerned.

"I just got a call from the crime lab,"

Steve said. "They've analyzed the bullets recovered from the parking structure this morning. They were .38 caliber slugs."

"What's so unusual about that?" Jack asked.

"It's not the bullets that are unusual," Steve said. "It's the gun they came from."

"So the lab was able to match the bullets to a previous crime," Mark said. "Isn't that good news?"

"Depends on how you look at it," Steve replied. "Whoever was shooting at you today was firing the same gun that was used ten years ago to kill a French tourist in San Francisco."

"Jean-Marc Gaddois," Mark said darkly.

Steve nodded, equally grim. Amanda took a seat, shaken by the news. A bewildered look passed between Jack and Jesse. They were obviously missing some vital piece of information, because they didn't see what was so shocking about all this.

"I don't understand, Mark," Jesse said. "How do you know about this French tourist?"

"Because he was supposedly the fifth victim of serial killer Randall Blore, who is currently serving several concurrent life sentences on death row," Mark explained. "I believe the tourist, and several other victims attributed to a string of serial killers, were actually killed by someone else, someone we're calling the Silent Partner."

"Now we know you were right," Amanda said. "At least about Gaddois."

"There's something else we know," Steve said, facing his dad. "The Silent Partner is back, and he knows you're onto him."

That was true. But it was also perplexing.

The killer had never acted so brazenly before, at least as far as Mark knew. Up until now, the Silent Partner had always been methodical about his crimes, careful to make sure that he was never seen and that there was little chance of being captured in the act. But this time, he'd tried to gun down his victim in broad daylight in front of dozens of potential witnesses, making no effort to disguise the crime as the work of someone else. There had to be easier ways to kill Mark with less risk of exposure.

So, why go after Mark this way? What had happened to change the killer's behavior? What had provoked him to give up his careful planning and go for a quick, almost panicked kill?

A thousand disparate facts were coalescing in Mark's mind, forming a new and very disturbing realization.

Now Mark knew, with absolute certainty, one more thing about the Silent Partner that he hadn't known before. And it scared him.

"We've found a sixth kill," Agent Terry Riordan said, standing at Mark Sloan's kitchen table, his unofficial field office. "A hitchhiker in Santa Cruz, two years ago. Her body was dumped at a campsite, like four other killings in the area. But her killing was the only one at which an Oakes Diet Root Beer bottle cap was collected at the scene, right beside the body."

"Where's Tanis?" Steve asked.

"She went home for a little shut-eye," Terry said. "She'd been up for thirty-six hours straight."

Mark glanced at his living room, surveying the agents working a case that, until a few days ago, nobody knew existed and that, until yesterday, had been his own personal obsession. Now there were files everywhere and a corkboard covered with crime scene photos and reports, and the investigation was widening with each passing hour.

He should have been pleased. Instead, he was worried.

"You know about the attempt on my life this morning," Mark said, "and about the bullets matching the ones recovered from the French tourist?"

"It's an exciting break in the case," Terry said. "And a strong validation of your instincts."

"It's more than that, I'm afraid." Mark motioned for Steve and Terry to follow him outside onto the deck, out of earshot of the other agents.

"What do all the murders have in common?" Mark asked them, once they were outside.

"They were made to look like another serial killer did them," Steve replied.

"And he did it without raising suspicion for years," Mark said. "The one thing we haven't asked ourselves was how he was able to do that."

"What do you mean?" Terry asked.

"He matched the details of the killings perfectly, mimicking the actions of several different serial killers so well that no one considered for even a second that they were copycat murders," Mark said. "Why didn't they?"

"Because the killer knew crucial details about the murders that hadn't been released to the press," Steve said, and then

228

came to the same, unsettling conclusion that his father had already had, back at the hospital.

"Which is an amazing feat to pull off," Mark said. "And he did it not just once, but several times that we know about. He knew every significant detail about the murders he copied. Unless he knew each serial killer personally, there's only one way he could have known so much."

Terry saw where Mark was headed, too, and he didn't like it. "You think he's a cop."

"Or an FBI agent," Steve added pointedly. "It could be anyone in law enforcement who was working those serial killer investigations or had access to the information back then."

"Not just then, but now," Mark said. "He knew his killings had finally been revealed. He knew to come after me. And there's only one way that's possible."

Mark turned and looked at the agents working in the living room, methodically going through the case files, and thought about what they represented.

"He's one of us."

Around midnight, Steve made a junk food run to the Trancas Market, which was across from the beach house on the other side of the Pacific Coast Highway.

The agents probably could have survived until morning without a fresh stock of chips, cookies and soft drinks, but they would have been grumpy about it. Steve was using the errand as an excuse to get some air and clear his head.

It was a chilly night, a fine layer of fog rolling in off the ocean and shrouding the parking lot in mist. Steve didn't bother wearing a jacket for the short walk. The cold air was refreshing after so many hours in the crowded living room, reading hundreds of pages of old typewritten reports.

They'd been painstakingly scrutinizing case files, analyzing computer records and compiling exhaustive lists of absolutely anybody who ever participated in any way in the investigation of the serial killings the Silent Partner chose to emulate.

The research was arduous and dull, but it had to be done, and done quickly. Already the master list of potential suspects was long and unwieldy and included detectives, uniformed officers, FBI agents, profilers, crime lab technicians, secretaries, dispatchers and coroners from all over the state and across the nation. They were even cross-checking the names of waitresses, cooks and delivery boys at all restaurants that cops ordered takeout from during the investigations. All the names were being inputted into the FBI's computer system, which they hoped would sort through the entries and reduce the hundreds of names to a handful of likely suspects.

Steve had no doubt that his father was right, that the killer was someone on the inside. He just hoped it ended up being a civilian employee instead of someone with a badge. If the Silent Partner turned out to be a cop, it would be a crushing blow to the department and it would shatter what little trust the community still had in the scandal-plagued LAPD.

He was pushing a cart down the potato chip aisle, trying to ignore the excruciating Muzak version of Madonna's "Like A Virgin" on the market's sound system, when he became aware of someone else standing nearby. The big man stood in the center of the aisle, like a frontier marshal preparing to draw on an outlaw.

"Evening, Chief," Steve said, trying to sound as casual as he could.

The chief stood in his perfectly-pressed suit and tie, his legs apart, his arms crossed under his broad chest, glowering at Steve like something disgusting he'd just stepped in.

"Tell me, Detective, do you enjoy being a police officer?"

"I did," Steve said.

If Chief Masters was amused, he certainly didn't show it. "I'm trying to understand whether you thought all of this through or just acted without thinking."

"A little of both, I suppose," Steve said, picking a bag of Nacho Cheese Doritos off the shelf and dropping it in his cart. He wanted to appear unperturbed and self-confident, even if he didn't feel that way.

"First you disobey my direct orders and undermine my authority by passing confidential files to a civilian," Masters said. "Then you go outside the department and share an internal situation with federal authorities."

"You didn't give me any choice."

"No, I didn't," the chief said firmly. "Because you don't make the choices; I do. Your job is to do as you are told by your commanding officer."

"Not if it means letting a murderer keep on killing," Steve said.

"What makes you think it does?"

"The evidence, sir."

The chief snorted derisively. "You're

willing to throw away your career on the strength of a bottle cap and a potato?"

"Someone tried to kill my father today," Steve said.

"I'm aware of that," the chief said. "I'm also aware it's not the first time that's happened."

"The bullets came from the same gun that Randall Blore supposedly used to kill a French tourist in San Francisco."

"And you think that proves Dr. Sloan's theory about another killer," Masters said. "The so-called Silent Partner?"

"Yes, I do," said Steve, trying hard not to show how surprised he was by how much the chief knew.

"All it proves, Detective, is that a weapon used in a murder was used again."

"It proves the tourist wasn't killed by Randall Blore."

"You'd like it to prove that, and you desperately *need* it to, or you have no career left. But the fact is, the gun doesn't prove anything," the chief said. "I worked that case, as you certainly know by now. Randall Blore used several weapons in his killing spree, but only one was recovered. Do you know what happened to those other weapons?"

"No, sir."

"Did it ever occur to you that perhaps one of Blore's friends or family members got wind of your father's investigation? That perhaps they took a shot at him with one of Blore's unrecovered guns to take advantage of the situation, to manufacture doubt about Blore's conviction?"

No, it hadn't occurred to him. And hearing it now sent a chill down Steve's spine. The chief noted Steve's discomfort.

"I didn't think so," Masters said. "You, your father and Lieutenant Archer are embarking on a foolhardy and dangerous course of action that could have very serious repercussions for this city."

"There could be worse repercussions if we don't," Steve said. "More people could die. We're committed now, Chief. We're going to see this through to the end, whatever it may be."

Chief Masters stared at Steve for a long, unsettling moment. Steve reached for a can of dip and dropped it in his cart just so he didn't look completely intimidated, which, of course, he was.

"You'd better hope that you're right, Detective," the chief said. "Because if you aren't, on behalf of the department and the citizens of this city, I'll make your lives a living hell."

And with that, the chief turned and walked slowly away.

Steve put the dip back on the shelf and continued his shopping. If he wasn't careful, he thought to himself, very soon he wouldn't be a customer here anymore. He'd be an employee.

The patient on the operating table the next morning was dead, but no one seemed to notice. The doctors and nurses were still treating him as if he were alive.

The patient was one of two cadavers supplied by Amanda to assist Mark in re-creating Stanley Tidewell's kidney transplant as accurately as possible.

Both surgical teams were reassembled in the same operating rooms as before. The operations were even being restaged at the same time of day as the original procedures. Video cameras were positioned in both operating rooms to catch anything Mark might miss during his personal observation.

Mark began in Jesse's surgical suite, watching the operation to remove the kidney from Billy Tidewell or, in this case, the corpse standing in for him. Amanda was in Jack's operating room, observing the concurrent medical procedures on the body that was standing in for Stanley Tidewell.

Jesse's surgical team consisted of anesthesiologist Dwight Tatum, scrub nurse Teresa Chingas, circulating nurse Susan Hilliard and Willie Armitage, the assistant surgeon.

Mark watched every move closely, asking himself how each seemingly ordinary function might be used to contaminate the organ with penicillin. Could it be on the surgeon's gloves? Could it be in the IV? Could it be on the instruments?

Mark tried to think like the killer, to ask himself how he could poison the kidney without being caught during, or after, the operation. A number of possibilities presented themselves, and he followed each one through in his mind as the surgery went forward.

He paid particular attention to Teresa Chingas and Dwight Tatum, each of whom had strong motives for sabotaging the operation and ruining Jack Stewart in the process.

Jesse sliced into the cadaver's abdomen. Once he entered the belly, he moved the intestines aside to give him access to the kidney. He clamped the renal artery and vein, then cut them and the ureter.

236

As Jesse was doing this, Mark watched the movements of the rest of the team. He studied Susan as she opened up instrument packs and prepared the saline solution for the blue plastic basin that would carry the kidney. He studied how Teresa handled the instruments she passed to Jesse. He examined the IV line, the syringes and the instruments. With each step, Mark saw opportunities for a killer to act and obstacles to his success.

As familiar as Mark was with transplant operations, the restaging was enormously helpful to him. The way each person worked, how they contributed to the operation and interacted with others, even where their hands were between tasks, were idiosyncratic and essential to understanding how the killer pulled off the murder.

But Mark knew it wasn't a totally accurate re-creation of events. The reenactment was a quiet, solemn affair, a distinct difference from the friendly, talkative atmosphere in the operating room during the original operation. The easy camaraderie, the sharing of hospital gossip and other small talk weren't happening again. This felt much more like a funeral.

While Mark accepted that it was impossible to recapture the atmosphere in the room, he did realize it was an important component. The typical workplace conversation was a natural distraction that would have made it far less likely that Jesse, or anyone else, would notice the seemingly insignificant actions of the killer at work.

Mark stepped in close as Jesse removed the kidney from the cadaver. Susan handed the plastic pan to Teresa, who held it out to Jesse, who gently placed the organ in it. Teresa poured the saline solution over the kidney from a sterile plastic bag. Mark followed Teresa as she carried the kidney to the adjoining operating room. She was alone, and out of sight, for less than ten seconds. Plenty of time to taint the kidney any number of ways.

They entered the other surgical suite. Jack had already opened up the cadaver and removed the bad kidney. He removed the new kidney from the pan, gently laid it into place in the cadaver and began the implantation procedure.

Mark and Amanda circulated around the operating room and observed as the steps of Billy Tidewell's surgery were essentially played out in reverse. A hundred possibilities for tampering with the organ ran through Mark's mind. Could the sutures be soaked in penicillin? If so, by whom and when? If the penicillin was in the IV, why didn't it show up in Stanley's blood?

The re-creation of Stanley Tidewell's implantation proceeded just as quietly and solemnly as the restaging of Billy Tidewell's kidney removal, except when it came time to replay Stanley's death. There was a palpable sense of sadness, desperation and, at least on Jack's part, anger. As Jack relived Stanley's death, he looked into the eyes of each person in the room, as if their culpability would somehow be revealed in their eyes. If it was, Jack missed it and so did Mark, Amanda and Jesse, who'd come to watch the second operation just as he had the day Stanley was murdered.

Afterwards, Mark remained in the operating room as it was broken down and cleaned. He stood in a corner, alone with his thoughts, watching as virtually everything except the instruments and clothing was dumped in biohazard bags, taken away and destroyed. That meant the gloves, bags, tubes, syringes, lines, drapes, sheets, fluids and pans were all gone. The surgical instruments went back to central supply for resterilization. The clothing the doctors and nurses wore was sent back to the laundry for cleaning. Any trace elements on the instruments or the clothing was long gone, thoroughly washed away. In essence, Mark not only watched a rerun of the murder but also the destruction of all his evidence.

But it didn't discourage him. Quite the contrary. It brought the facts into sharper focus. He replayed both operations through in his mind once more, considered everything all the suspects had said and evaluated their actions before and after the murder.

Then all the seemingly unrelated facts snapped into place in his mind like Lego blocks, building a solid structure of events that he could visualize and examine from all angles.

Mark left the operating room knowing how the murder was committed and who the killer had to be. He didn't want to believe it, but the truth was inescapable.

And one way or another, despite how difficult the truth was for him to accept, he'd find a way to prove it.

CHAPTER SEVENTEEN

"We have to make this go away."

It was Clarke Trotter's mantra, and Mark wasn't surprised that it was the first thing the hospital's general counsel said to him as he entered the attorney's office. Mark had rushed up from the blood lab as soon as he received Trotter's urgent page.

"Did you know the Tidewell family is suing us for thirty million dollars?" Trotter asked.

Mark nodded. "I can't say I'm surprised, given the circumstances."

"A lawsuit like this could ruin our reputation in the community that gave us our name," said Trotter, pulling on his tie as he spoke, as if it would somehow make it long enough and wide enough to cover his considerable beer belly. "If word gets out about Dr. Stewart's incompetence, admissions could drop off significantly. One doctor's mistakes can tarnish the entire hospital."

"This isn't a case of medical malpractice," Mark said. "I believe it's murder."

"Oh, that will go over so much better. Bloodthirsty doctors are much more acceptable than incompetent ones," Trotter said sarcastically. "Frankly, Dr. Sloan, it's astonishing to me we have any patients left after the notoriety you've brought this hospital."

"What is that supposed to mean?" Mark felt his cheeks reddening with anger.

"Let's just say that your 'extracurricular activities' have endangered the staff, the patients and the hospital itself on many occasions," Trotter said. "Need I remind you that half this hospital was reduced to rubble because of your actions?"

"I didn't set off that bomb," Mark argued.

"No, you antagonized a serial bomber, making yourself and this hospital a target. Just like yesterday, when our parking structure was turned into a shooting gallery," Trotter said. "Neither of these events would have happened if you were simply doing your job as chief of internal medicine instead of indulging your other pursuits as well."

Mark took a deep breath. He didn't want to say anything out of anger that he would regret later. "My other pursuits, as you put it, have nothing to do with Stanley Tidewell's murder."

"Community Healthcorp International owns five other hospitals in the United States besides Community General. We haven't had a single murder or bombing or drive-by shooting at our other hospitals," Trotter said. "And yet here, where one of our doctors dabbles in homicide investigations, we've had all three." Trotter smoothed out his tie again. "Have you considered going into private practice?"

Before Mark could respond, his beeper went off. It was a 911 from Steve. Mark guessed it meant there had been an important new development in the Silent Partner investigation.

"We'll have to continue this discussion later," Mark said, rising from his chair.

"We certainly will," Trotter replied. "In the meantime, I'm going to arrange a settlement conference with Tidewell's lawyers before this embarrassing episode goes public."

"Let me know," Mark replied. "I want to be there."

Mark marched out of Trotter's office and headed for the elevator. Meeting with Trotter always made Mark angry. The lawyer put business before medicine and approached everything with mean-spirited sarcasm. But Mark had to concede the really irritating thing about Trotter was that there was often more than a little truth to what he said. This time that was especially true.

There was no denying that Mark frequently, and involuntarily, made himself a potential target for killers who wanted him off their trail. And by putting himself in danger, he was, by extension, endangering the lives of those around him, particularly the staff and patients at Community General, where he spent most of his time.

But by the same token, he was endangering people everywhere he went, whether it was the hospital, the gas station or the grocery store.

Did that mean he should abandon his pursuit of murderers? Or, if he continued, abandon medicine and live a life of complete seclusion?

Mark spent many sleepless nights wrestling with those issues and had come to a decision he could live with, though not without some lingering doubts and persistent guilt.

He believed if he gave up homicide investigation, or secluded himself, then the killers won. He couldn't let fear for himself, or others, stop him from bringing murderers to justice, even if law enforcement wasn't his official, or even principal, profession.

Even so, Trotter's argument struck a nerve and inflamed the guilt Mark often felt but tried to deny. But he knew he'd feel even greater guilt if people died at the hands of a murderer he'd failed to stop.

Which brought the Silent Partner investigation back to mind. What was the emergency?

When Mark walked into his living room, the FBI agents were still working the phones, the files and their computers, all pointedly doing their best to ignore the argument raging in the kitchen between Steve, Tanis and Agent Riordan.

The three stood at the kitchen table over a set of blueprints as Mark approached.

"We need to step back and reassess the situation before moving forward," Terry said. "I think we're jumping to conclusions here."

"There is nothing to reassess," Steve replied. "We have to strike now, before he has a chance to make another move."

"You're already talking about taking him down and I'm not sold that he's our guy,"

Terry said. "At most, we should sit down and have a talk with him, which we can arrange with a phone call instead of an armed assault."

"You call him, he's gone," Steve said, "if he isn't already."

Mark cleared his throat to get their attention. "Do you want to tell me what's going on?"

"We've had a major break in the case," Tanis replied.

"That remains to be seen," Terry interjected.

"We went through the lists of FBI and LAPD personnel who worked the serial killer cases that the Silent Partner copied," Steve explained. "We even cross-checked the information with names in the index of Freddy Meeks' books."

"In the interests of full disclosure," Tanis said, "my name shows up on two of the cases, Terry's on four, and Chief Masters, back when he was a lowly homicide detective, was an investigating officer on nearly all of them."

"That's what I mean," Terry said. "It could be you or even Chief Masters."

"Or you," Tanis added. "For the sake of argument, of course."

"My point is, we've barely scratched the

surface here," Terry said, pointedly ignoring her dig. "There may even be some low-level clerical worker who's escaped our initial pass who had some kind of access to all the investigations."

"But there's only one significant player who shows up across the board," Steve said firmly. "And he's the only one besides Tanis, the chief and you who'd know that my father had discovered the Silent Partner."

Mark considered the facts, and Agent Riordan's reluctance to act, and made a simple deduction about who they were talking about. It was a nightmare.

"It's Lou Rozan," Mark said. "The FBI profiler."

The man they counted on to give them an accurate picture of serial killers was one himself. But it made frightening sense to Mark. Who better to emulate killers than the man who knew them best?

"I don't think so," Terry said tersely. "It's a major reach."

"He was assigned to all the cases except the Traveler investigation," Tanis argued, referring to the serial killer who picked up hitchhikers and stabbed them to death.

"There you go," Terry said. "Lou doesn't actually fit the pattern we were looking for. He wasn't involved in all the investigations."

"But we can place him in Las Vegas when the killing of the hitchhiker in Baker took place," Tanis said. "He was attending an annual convention of criminalists and profilers."

"So what? Being in an adjacent state isn't enough to make him a suspect," Terry said. "Nor does it prove he knew key details of the Traveler investigation."

"C'mon, Terry," Steve said. "Even if he wasn't working the Traveler case, he certainly had unrestricted access to the investigation. No one would have thought twice about letting him look through whatever he wanted. He was one of your top profilers."

"Which is why this whole discussion is ridiculous," Terry replied. "I don't see a guy who puts serial killers away being one himself."

"Or you don't want to," Mark replied. "The fact is, neither do I. But maybe the reason he understands serial killers so well is because he is one himself."

"I could say the same about you, Dr. Sloan."

"Lou was also working with us on the chief's task force on unsolved homicides,"

Tanis said. "He tried to bury the Lydia Yates file from the beginning."

"So did the chief," Terry said. "I don't see you talking about arresting him."

"The chief couldn't have been in the car that came after Mark yesterday," Tanis said. "He was at a breakfast seminar on community policing with a couple hundred civic leaders."

"Look, I'm not saying there isn't stuff to pursue here; I just don't want us rushing to judgment before all the facts are in," Terry said. "Let's spend some more time going through the files, make sure we didn't miss someone else, someone who makes more sense for this."

"Someone who isn't an FBI agent," Mark said.

"I didn't say that," Terry snapped back.

"You didn't have to," Mark said. "You assembled this strike force because you saw an opportunity to embarrass the LAPD and be rewarded for your initiative. But if the killer turns out to be an FBI profiler, then the bureau will ultimately end up looking worse than the department. And you certainly don't want to be the agent responsible for that. Now you find yourself in a politically untenable position."

"I got into this to stop a killer," Terry said defensively. "Politics never entered into it."

"Well, it certainly has now," Tanis said. "You wouldn't be hesitating if the evidence pointed to a cop."

"There is a way to minimize the damage and spare both the LAPD and the FBI some embarrassment," Mark said. "You move forward officially as a joint LAPD/ FBI operation. That way, no single agency gets the credit or the blame for Lou Rozan's crimes going undetected. But if you don't get a warrant and move on Rozan right now, I'll go to the chief myself. You and I both know that given these new facts, he'll jump on this now."

Terry hesitated, clearly weighing his options. Mark decided to give him one more to consider.

"How do you think it will look when an FBI agent is arrested by the LAPD for murder?"

Terry frowned and stared past them out to the beach. A couple days ago, this looked like a no-risk bet, a golden opportunity to jump-start his unremarkable career by giving the bureau a public relations victory and scoring a high-profile prosecution for himself. Now, instead of becoming a star, he would be lucky if he came out of this with his career where it was when he started. But Mark was right; he didn't have much choice.

"Okay, Dr. Sloan, we'll do this your way," Terry said. "But what happens when you're wrong, and Lou Rozan isn't our guy?"

"We start again," Mark said.

"Won't happen," Terry said. "The damage will already be done. The bureaucrats will take over and bury everything, including the three of us. There will never be another investigation into this."

"It's a risk I'm willing to take," Mark said.

"And one you're forcing all of us to take with you," Terry replied, glancing between Steve and Tanis. "Think about that."

"The way I see it," Steve said, "I'm just doing my job."

"You're suspended," Tanis said with a smile. "Technically, you don't have a job."

Steve smiled back. "I meant I'm doing my job the way I'd do it if I still had a job."

"Oh," Tanis said. "Since you put it that way, so am I."

Terry glanced at them both and sighed. The battle was over and he'd lost.

"We'll take him down tonight at his

house. But if Lou is guilty, he's not going to open the door and invite us in, warrant or not," Terry said. "I've seen him in action. He's one tough son of a bitch. He won't go down without a fight."

"That's why I took the liberty of pulling the blueprints for his house," Steve said, unfurling the plans on the table.

Mark studied the drawings and was impressed by the thought that had gone into them. It had nothing to do with aesthetics. It was the functionality.

This was clearly the home of a man who understood the way a killer thinks and who fully expected to become a target of violence himself.

But it was more than that.

It was a blueprint for death. It was a warning to anyone who dared attack him.

You'll die trying.

CHAPTER EIGHTEEN

The land around Lou Rozan's one-story, ranch style house in the northern San Fernando Valley had been graded as flat as a putting green and was just as well manicured. All the trees had been removed, leaving a wide green belt between the house and the tall wrought-iron fence, which was blanketed with thorny climbing roses. The entire property was protected by an elaborate alarm- and video-surveillance system. Motion-activated floodlights ringed the house. Anything larger than a rat that tried to cross the lawn would be instantly bathed in light with no place to hide from Rozan's gunsights.

But if all that failed and the house was breached, Rozan could always retreat to a virtually impregnable safe room, where he had air, food, water, weapons, communications and complete control of the house, which might also include any number of booby traps.

Any attempt to go in and get Rozan

could become a prolonged, and bloody, siege.

But none of that concerned Mark as much as what the FBI discovered on their initial drive-by recon of Rozan's house early in the evening.

The smashed Honda sedan that pursued Mark in the parking structure was parked on Rozan's driveway in plain view behind the gate.

"This isn't good," Terry Riordan said, as he, Steve, Tanis and a dozen other agents suited up in bulletproof Kevlar vests outside the command van, which was parked two blocks away from Rozan's house.

Agents had already sealed off the streets leading to the house and cleared Rozan's immediate neighbors from their homes. Mark doubted the evacuation went unnoticed by Rozan, who by now certainly knew company was coming. And judging by the car parked out front, Rozan had been expecting them for some time.

"It means he doesn't give a damn if we know," Steve said. "He's hunkering down for a fight."

"Or he's given up," Mark said.

"Have you seen that fortress he lives in?" Terry said. "Does that strike you as the home of a quitter?"

Mark glanced down the street at Rozan's house, which was hidden from view, set back behind the dense wall of roses.

"Then it wouldn't hurt to give him a call and see if we can talk him out of a firefight," Mark said.

Steve and Terry shared a look; then Terry handed Mark a cell phone. "Knock yourself out."

Mark dialed Rozan's number. He let it ring a dozen times before giving up, flipping the phone shut and handing it back to Terry.

"I guess he's not in the mood to talk," Mark said. "So what's your strategy?"

"We'll try the simple way first," Steve said. "We'll ring the bell and see if he'll let us in."

"And if he doesn't?" Mark asked.

Terry motioned to an FBI urban assault vehicle parked down the street. It looked like a streamlined tank with a battering ram instead of a gun turret. The navy blue paint and FBI insignia on the vehicle did little to blunt its militaristic intent.

"We drive that through the fence and right into his living room," Terry said.

"Isn't that a little extreme?" Mark asked.

"He didn't give us an alternative," Tanis said. "The grass around his house is a kill zone. He could pick us off with ease if we tried to cross it."

Mark reached into the command truck, grabbed a Kevlar vest and began to strap it on.

"What do you think you're doing?" Steve said.

"Getting dressed for a house call," Mark said.

FBI agents took positions outside the fence that surrounded the house, just in case Rozan had some hidden exit from which he could escape. Sharpshooters stationed themselves on the rooftops of the neighboring houses and took aim, ready to provide cover if necessary.

Steve, Mark and Tanis approached the front gate, the only exposed portion of the fence. Steve and Tanis had their guns drawn, ready for anything. Through the wrought-iron slats, they could see the Honda parked on the driveway, leaking oil like blood. All seemed quiet. Nothing moved behind the closed shutters of the house.

There was an intercom and a bell beside the gate. Mark pressed the bell. There was no response. Mark started to step in front of the gate, but Steve pulled him back.

"Dad, don't," Steve said. "You're making

yourself a clean target."

Mark looked over his shoulder at the sharpshooters, then turned back to Steve. "I think I'm safe."

Mark stepped in front of the gate and faced the house. "Lou, it's Mark Sloan," he shouted. "I'd like to talk with you."

He waited a moment, but there was no sign that anyone in the house had heard.

"As you know by now, the police and FBI are here. They have a warrant to search your house," Mark shouted. "I know you're a reasonable man, Lou. We can do this without anybody getting hurt."

Mark stared at the house, hoping for some kind of sign and getting none. He stepped away from the gate and sighed.

"I wish it didn't have to come to this," Mark said to Steve.

"Me too, Dad." Steve clicked his radio and spoke to the tactical team. "Let's take him."

The FBI's urban assault vehicle rumbled down the street, past the well-tended yards with their Toyotas in the driveway, basketball hoops above the garage and children's toys on the grass. It reminded Mark that underneath even the most peaceful exterior, the potential for violence always lurked.

The tank pivoted sharply and headed straight for the wrought-iron fence, Terry Riordan leading a phalanx of armed FBI agents behind the vehicle, using it for cover.

The front-mounted battering ram slammed into the fence, tearing through the tangle of thorns and smashing through the wrought-iron slats, followed an instant later by the full body of the vehicle. The fence folded under the tank with a loud iron squeal that sounded like a primitive wail of agony.

The floods around the perimeter of the house immediately flashed on, illuminating the entire yard in harsh white light. Steve, Mark and Tanis fell into step beside the FBI agents, following the deep tracks the tank chewed into the manicured lawn.

The tank punched a hole through the house as if the walls were made of Styrofoam. Steve, Tanis and the agents scrambled through the jagged opening into the house. Mark waited anxiously on the grass, bracing himself for the sound of gunfire, relieved when he didn't hear any and yet strangely unnerved by the silence. He didn't move until he heard Terry yell that it was all clear.

Mark carefully climbed over the rubble

into the house and stopped when he saw the scene in the living room. He wasn't surprised. It was a possibility he'd considered ever since he'd learned the Honda was parked in the driveway.

Lou Rozan sat in a leather easy chair, a Smith and Wesson .38 in his hand, the top of his head blown off, blood splattered across the wall.

He'd killed himself.

As much as Mark loathed Rozan for the crimes he committed, he was saddened by the suicide. With Rozan's death went any possibility of ever truly knowing how many murders he'd committed and understanding the motivation behind his horrible crimes.

What kind of man helped capture serial killers and at the same time emulated them? Was he a killer before he became a profiler? Or did he crawl so deep into the minds of the murderers he pursued that he transformed into one himself?

Unfortunately, they'd never know. The Silent Partner had lived up to his name, even in death.

Mark slipped on a pair of rubber gloves and knelt in front of the body, examining the grisly crime scene. No matter how many times Mark witnessed the ugly aftermath of violent death, he never got used to it.

From what he could tell from the obvious physical signs, the blond-haired, blue-eyed agent had been dead for at least a day. It appeared he'd put the gun to his temple and pulled the trigger. Rozan's right arm hung over the edge of the chair, the gun dangling from his index finger.

Mark looked around Lou's body for a note but didn't see one. That didn't surprise him, either. He doubted Rozan felt sorry for what he'd done, only sorry that he'd finally been caught.

There was an empty wineglass on the table and a bottle of Chardonnay that had toppled and spilled on the floor. Lying beside the wine was a prescription pill bottle and a dozen oblong white tablets that had spilled out of it.

Mark picked up the pill bottle and read the prescription label. It was Xanax, and it was prescribed for Lou Rozan by Dr. Roger Philby, who was undoubtedly his psychiatrist, one who would soon be questioning himself about how good he was at his job.

The bloody scene in front of Mark told a clear story. Rozan knew his world was closing in on him. His desperate assassination attempt on Mark had failed, and it was only a matter of time before the authorities showed up at his door. So Rozan sat down with a nice glass of wine and a couple of Xanax. And when he felt nice and relaxed and at peace with himself, he put the gun to his temple and blew his brains out.

"You had him pegged, Dr. Sloan," Terry Riordan said as he approached. "He gave up. At least the bastard saved us, and the victims' families, from a long trial and a media circus."

And, Mark thought, any further embarrassment for the bureau or the LAPD. Perhaps that was why Rozan had killed himself, out of some twisted sense of loyalty to the bureau that had somehow managed to endure despite his killing spree.

Mark stood up and strode to the front door. It was unlocked. The alarm panel beside the door indicated that the security system was unarmed. Lou had all but invited them to come in. Terry Riordan could have left his tank in the garage.

Steve called out to Mark from the kitchen. "Dad, you better come look at this."

Mark stepped into the kitchen, which had been lovingly restored to its original

1960s condition. Even the refrigerator Steve was standing beside was either a reproduction or a rebuilt model from the same era.

Steve stepped aside to let his Dad look inside the refrigerator. It was packed with fruits, vegetables, juice, a couple bottles of wine and several six-packs of Oakes Diet Root Beer.

Tanis came in, peeling off the Velcro straps of her Kevlar vest. "I just checked his office. He's got complete files on all the serial killer cases we've been looking at and dozens of others. It could be months before we know just how many murders this bastard committed."

"We may never know," Mark said.

"At least he won't be killing any more," Steve said, holstering his weapon.

Mark usually felt a sense of satisfaction when a mystery was solved and a killer stopped, but not this time. He realized now that Lou Rozan controlled the way the case had played out right down to the endgame. Rozan killed as many people as he wanted, and when the authorities finally noticed, he decided where and when his fun would end.

If anything, Mark and the others were just peripheral players in a drama Rozan wrote, produced and directed. They couldn't even say that justice had been served. The Silent Partner robbed them of that with a bullet. It was Rozan's final, bitter act of control.

When it came right down to it, Mark thought, Lou Rozan had beaten them all.

The Silent Partner investigation was about to shift into a new phase, from apprehension to comprehension. Who was Lou Rozan? When did he begin killing? How many people did he kill in his lifetime? Who were the victims and why were they chosen? To answer those questions, and hundreds more, they would begin backtracking their way through his life, tracing his movements from the time he learned how to walk. But before that painstaking process could begin, there was still one more formality.

The autopsy.

Mark, Steve and Terry reconvened at two a.m. in the Adjunct County Medical Examiner's morgue at Community General Hospital to hear Dr. Amanda Bentley's preliminary findings. When they got there, there was already someone besides Amanda, and Lou Rozan's corpse, waiting for them.

Chief John Masters stood stoically in a dark corner, arms folded across his chest, staring down at the body on the table.

Amanda wasn't used to such a large audience, but she realized this was not only an autopsy of the victim but of the investigation as well. This was the beginning of what would be a very, very long journey for all of them. The cases against each of the serial killers that the Silent Partner mimicked would now be resurrected and painstakingly reinvestigated from scratch by every arm of law enforcement, including her office. No doubt every single one of the incarcerated killers he emulated would appeal their convictions, creating a judicial logjam in the courts for years to come.

That unpleasant prospect, and the inevitable political fallout, certainly explained the scowl on Chief Masters' face, Amanda thought. That, and the embarrassment of being proved wrong by an insubordinate detective, an irritating civilian and the FBI. She wondered if the chief knew of her own role in Mark's investigation, and if he did, what kind of retribution she could look forward to.

With all that in mind, she cleared her throat and began her report.

"The victim was killed by a single, self-inflicted gunshot wound to the right temple, as characterized by the stellate entry pattern," she said, pointing to the wound. "The bullet exited the skull and was recovered from the wall."

"Ballistics confirm the bullet came from the same gun used in the killing of the French tourist and the attempted murder of Dr. Sloan," Terry added.

"The angle of entry indicates the gun was fired by the victim, which is confirmed by gunpowder residue on his right hand and sleeve," she continued. "Pooling of the blood in the body indicates that the victim was killed where he sat and that the death occurred about thirty-six hours ago. Blood, urine and tissue analysis reveals the victim consumed three milligrams of alprazolam, also known as Xanax, immediately prior to his death, most likely in conjunction with several glasses of wine on a nearly empty stomach, which would considerably heighten the effects of the medication."

"Xanax is a short-acting sedative that is commonly prescribed to treat anxiety disorders," Mark explained. "Rozan's usual dosage was point two five milligrams, twice a day."

"According to Rozan's shrink," Terry said, "he was being treated for post-traumatic stress disorder and seemed to be showing, and I quote, 'remarkable progress.'"

"I'd say he's cured now," Steve said wryly.

"The Xanax didn't directly contribute to his death, nor was it by any means a lethal dosage," Amanda said. "It's quite common for suicide victims to take drugs or alcohol to steady their nerves or dull their senses before taking their own lives. That's all I've got, unless you have any questions."

"I think you've covered everything, Dr. Bentley," the chief said. "Would you excuse us, please?"

"Certainly, Chief." Amanda nodded politely and gladly left the room. Being around Masters always made her nervous.

As soon as she was gone, the chief stepped out of the shadows and into the circle of light around the examination table.

"I'd like to hear the evidence," the chief said.

Steve and Terry recapped Mark's initial findings, the subsequent discovery of two other killings that could be linked to the Silent Partner and finally the narrowing down of suspects to those few people who had access to both the original serial-killer investigations and knowledge of Mark's recent discoveries.

"We were able to positively link the car in Rozan's driveway to the shooting at Community General," Steve said. "We also found a substantive link to the Lydia Yates murder. The position of the driver's seat was seventeen inches from the gas pedal, just like the driver's seat in her car."

"Rozan had copies of case files in his possession on all the serial-killer investigations that the Silent Partner emulated," Terry said. "The son of a bitch also had files on dozens of other active and inactive serial-killer cases. We're going through them now, looking for any other possible murders Rozan might have committed."

"We found bottles of Oakes Diet Root Beer in his refrigerator," Steve said. "And just for kicks we examined his fruits and vegetables. They were all organic, like the potato used in the French tourist's killing."

"Everything is circumstantial except the gun," the chief said.

"We've convicted people on a lot less, not that we have to worry about that this time," Terry said. "Rozan solved that problem for us."

The chief nodded, then looked up at Mark. "Satisfied, Doctor?"

"I don't get any pleasure out of this, Chief," Mark said. "I'm just relieved that it's over."

"It's far from over, Dr. Sloan," the chief said, striding towards the door. "I will see you all at the press conference tomorrow morning at ten a.m."

Mark followed Masters into the deserted hospital corridor. "One more thing, Chief."

Masters turned and looked down at Mark. "Yes, Doctor?"

"What happens to my son and Tanis Archer?"

"Nothing's changed," the chief said. "There will be an internal affairs investigation into their misconduct."

"Thanks to their actions, we ended a killing spree that might otherwise have continued unnoticed for years."

"The ends do not justify the means, Doctor."

"In this case," Mark said, "I think they do."

"You aren't the chief of police."

"You won't be either if I go public about your efforts to shut down the investigation, which I will do if Steve and Tanis are penalized in any way for the help they gave me."

The chief met Mark's defiant gaze. "Are you blackmailing me, Dr. Sloan?"

"That's what it sounds like, doesn't it?" Mark said.

The chief stared at Mark a moment longer, then turned and walked away without saying another word.

CHAPTER NINETEEN

It was six a.m. by the time the FBI agents finished carting out all their files, furniture and equipment, which were being taken to a conference room at the Federal Building, where the joint LAPD/FBI task force would be based for the next phase of the Silent Partner investigation.

Mark didn't bother trying to get any sleep, not with all the activity in the house and the press conference scheduled in just a few hours.

Instead, Mark and Steve dragged their furniture back into the living room and straightened the house up, hardly speaking as they worked, their minds still on Lou Rozan and his string of murders.

They both showered and changed, then met again in the kitchen for a quick, simple breakfast of cereal, milk and coffee.

"I'm still trying to figure Lou Rozan out," Steve said.

"It's going to take a lot longer than a couple hours, Steve," Mark said. "I'm sure people will be studying his case for years to come."

"I have a hard time understanding how a serial killer could become an FBI profiler," Steve said. "It's much easier for me to see how a profiler might become a killer. He spends every day of his life trying to get inside their heads, to understand the way they think, and then finally succeeds by becoming a killer himself."

"I think you're partly right," Mark said. "He didn't become *one* killer, he became *every* killer that he pursued; that's how he was able to catch them."

"So, you think that's why his killings were indistinguishable from the murders committed by the people he was chasing? Not because he was intentionally covering up his crimes to avoid detection?"

"Exactly," Mark said.

"That doesn't explain why he left a bottle cap behind at the scene of each of his murders."

"No, it doesn't," Mark admitted. "I'm not sure why he did that. Maybe, deep down, he wanted to get caught."

"Let's say you're right about why he was killing," Steve said. "How did he justify it to himself afterwards?"

"I'm not sure that he did," Mark said.

"He became desensitized to what he was doing; it was all about catching the serial killer he was hunting."

"I don't buy it, Dad." Steve shook his head. "On some level he understood what he was doing, or he wouldn't have had his breakdown, left the FBI and sought psychiatric help."

Mark thought about the case that led Rozan to resign from the FBI and escape into private sector security work. He'd been pursuing a child killer who mutilated and sexually molested his victims.

"Perhaps when it came time to kill a child in the same horrible way the serial killer had done, Rozan couldn't go through with it," Mark said. "He just snapped."

"Or he actually committed one of those murders and couldn't live with himself afterwards."

That was a disturbing possibility that Mark didn't even want to think about.

"I spoke to Dr. Philby, his psychiatrist," Steve said. "Rozan first came to him tortured by nightmares that were so vivid, he couldn't distinguish them from reality."

"He was talking about his killings, trying to cope with what he'd done," Mark said. "But it came out sounding like a textbook example of post-traumatic stress disorder."

"It took months of in-depth counseling and lots of medication before Rozan got the night terrors and flashbacks under control. The shrink really thought Rozan had conquered his anxieties."

"My guess is that the counseling and the medication allowed Rozan to see clearly for the first time what he'd been doing and what he'd become," Mark said. "The only way he could live with his crimes was to forgive himself, to believe he wasn't in control of his actions."

"I don't think so," Steve said. "If he truly believed that, he wouldn't have tried to kill you. That was the act of a desperate man afraid of being caught and punished for his crimes."

"You're right, Steve," Mark said, sighing. "We can spend the rest of our lives trying to figure him out and I doubt the pieces will ever fit snugly together."

That reminded Mark of one case where almost everything did fit, and that was Stanley Tidewell's murder. Mark knew who the murderer was, but there was still a missing piece of the puzzle he needed. Steve could find it for him.

"I need you to do me a favor today after the press conference," Mark said.

"Sure," Steve said. "What do you need?"

"I'd like you to talk to some bookies for me."

Steve grinned. "Feeling lucky?"

"Just hedging my bets," Mark said, and then explained what he wanted Steve to find out for him.

The LAPD press room at Parker Center was packed with reporters from every publication and broadcast outlet in the city. Although there had been no official comment from police yet, rumors were traveling fast and had already been reported on the morning newscasts.

The press knew that a major assault had been conducted in a residential neighborhood in the valley, and that one FBI agent was dead. They knew the assault was part of a major law enforcement operation involving a serial killer. That alone would have been newsworthy, but what they were about to learn would shock even the most hardened and experienced reporters in the room.

Mark wondered if Mike and Ken were in the crowd, or if they were broadcasting from a giant bucket of excrement somewhere, waiting for the news.

Chief Masters entered the room in his uniform blues, flanked by FBI Special

Agent Terry Riordan and several deputy chiefs and bureau officials. Mark and Steve followed close behind.

It had been decided, after especially tense negotiations between the chief and the director of the FBI in Washington, D.C., that the chief would make the initial remarks, followed by Special Agent Riordan.

"Thank you all for coming," the chief said. "At approximately eight forty-five p.m. last night, a joint LAPD/FBI task force served a search warrant on a home on the twenty-three hundred block of Sprague Street in Granada Hills in connection with an ongoing homicide investigation. The owner of the home, Louis Arthur Rozan, was discovered dead, the victim of a self-inflicted gunshot wound."

At the mention of Rozan's name, reporters began shouting out questions, drowning each other out. The chief raised his hands, motioning the reporters to quiet down.

"We'll get to your questions at the conclusion of our remarks," the chief said. "Louis Rozan was a former profiler for the FBI and for over a decade assisted federal, state and local law enforcement agencies in the investigation of serial killings, including the Reaper and Traveler cases, among others. Based on information initially unearthed by Dr. Mark Sloan and subsequent evidence developed by a joint LAPD/FBI task force, we now believe that Mr. Rozan committed at least half a dozen murders, which he disguised as crimes committed by those he was investigating."

Almost immediately the reporters started shouting out questions again, but the chief just stood there stoically, waiting them out. Finally the reporters got the message and fell silent. Mark had never seen anything like it. The power of the chief's physical presence was impressive, and he certainly knew how to use it.

"I would like to introduce FBI special agent Terence Riordan, who jointly headed the task force with LAPD homicide detective Steve Sloan." The chief surrendered the podium to Terry, who stepped up to the mike.

The agent was visibly nervous, unaccustomed to facing the press. He barely looked up from his notes as he spoke. The contrast between him and the chief wasn't lost on anybody, least of all the chief.

"I would like to thank Chief Masters for extending to the FBI the full resources of the Los Angeles Police Department during the course of this difficult and complex investigation," Terry said. "This task force is just one example of the smooth and effective interagency cooperation occurring each day between federal and local law enforcement. Together with the LAPD, we will be reopening every serial-killer investigation that Lou Rozan was involved with. We want to assure the public that we share their profound shock and sadness, and that the full scope of this man's crimes will be uncovered and justice will be served."

Terry stepped back and the chief stepped into his place.

"We'll take a few questions," the chief said.

A hundred reporters spoke at once, but one voice managed to rise above the cacophony.

"Do you expect this revelation to result in the release of scores of convicted serial killers?" the reporter shouted.

"No, I do not," the chief replied curtly, immediately shifting his attention to another reporter before the first one could follow up with another question.

"Did you know Lou Rozan was a suspected serial killer when you appointed him to your unsolved crimes task force?" the other reporter asked.

"Let me just say that this investigation has been ongoing for some time," the chief replied, and pointed to another reporter.

The questions continued for another twenty minutes, and got gradually more pointed, while the chief and, to a lesser degree Agent Riordan, fielded them with the vaguest possible responses. Mark had to marvel at the chief's skill at saying absolutely nothing while appearing to say a lot. But over the coming weeks and months, as all the details eventually came out, it would be much harder for the chief to maintain that posture. Masters' future as the next mayor of Los Angeles was hardly assured.

Mark and Steve got through the experience without having to say a word, which was fine with them both. When the press conference concluded, they followed the chief and Agent Riordan out a side door into a restricted corridor not open to the press.

Terry wiped the sweat from his brow. "Those lights are hot as hell."

"You better buy yourself some sunscreen, Agent Riordan," the chief said. "It only gets hotter."

Terry turned to Steve. "We should be heading back to the Federal Building.

There's a ton of paperwork we have to get through."

"Detective Sloan will not be joining you. He's returning to his duties in homicide," the chief said, glancing at Steve. "Unless you have an objection."

"No, sir," said Steve, who was glad simply to have his job back.

The chief shifted his attention again to Terry. "Deputy Chief Bishop is already at the Federal Building and will be coordinating our end of the investigation from this point on."

"Great," Terry said, then offered his hand to Steve. "Let's keep in touch."

Steve shook Terry's hand but considering the glare the chief was giving him, thought it best to offer nothing more than a noncommittal smile.

Terry immediately realized his mistake and rather than compound it, left it at that and walked away. The chief glowered at Steve, who was still standing there.

"What are you waiting for, Detective?" the chief asked. "Directions back to your office?"

"No, sir." Steve shot a quick glance at Mark, then went on his way.

Finally, the chief looked down at Mark, who hadn't made a move to go, and sighed heavily. "Is there something on your mind, Doctor?"

"I didn't see Tanis Archer at the press conference," Mark replied. "I was just wondering where she is."

"Exactly where she was before all this began," the chief said, turning to go. "Just like you asked."

Perhaps it was fitting that the Silent Partner investigation was ending for Mark the way it began, with a long, lonely walk through the dank subbasement of Parker Center to room D-127.

He entered to find Tanis Archer sitting at the wobbly card table with Freddy Meeks, both of them nursing cups of coffee under the dim yellow glow of the single lightbulb dangling from the ceiling. As usual, Freddy looked like he just got out of bed, his hair askew, wearing a wrinkled cable-knit sweater over a T-shirt. Tanis also looked tired and disheveled, but it was a new look for her. Mark figured his appearance wasn't much better.

Tanis waved him in.

"Welcome to the Blue Ribbon Task Force on Unsolved Homicides," Tanis said. "We're a little short of manpower right now. One of our guys got kicked off for stealing confidential files; the other was a serial killer."

"It would be funny if it wasn't so sad," Freddy said, finishing his coffee and crumpling his paper cup. There was a notepad in front of him, filled with handwriting.

"I'm surprised to see you down here," Mark said to Freddy.

"Where else would I be?" Freddy scratched the back of his neck, closed his notebook and slid his pencil into the spiral rings.

"I expected to see you at the press conference," Mark said. "Standing in the front row."

"I'm not a reporter anymore," Freddy said. "Besides, there was nothing to learn upstairs. I knew talking with Tanis would be a lot more interesting."

"He's been interrogating me about Lou for an hour," Tanis said. "I don't think he believes he did it."

Mark pulled out a chair and sat down, his eyes drawn to the seat Lou Rozan once filled.

"It's hard for me to accept, too," Mark said.

"*You* think it's hard?" Freddy asked, scratching his arm. "I knew the guy for years and never had an inkling. Here I am, writing one book after another about serial killers, and I don't recognize the one sitting right next to me."

"Don't be too hard on yourself, Freddy," Mark said. "No one saw it."

"It's different for me, Mark. I'm not saying he was my best friend or anything, but we worked closely together," Freddy said. "We also hung out sometimes after he left the bureau, when he was trying to get his life back together. I thought I really knew him."

"It's pretty unusual for a cop and a reporter to become buddies," Tanis said. "How did you guys manage it?"

"We met while I was a reporter, covering the police beat. I was always straight with him; he never got burned by me," Freddy said. "It worked both ways. All cops use the press, spreading misinformation to protect their cases or smoke out a killer. The difference with Lou was that he'd tell me when he was doing it. I always knew when I was being used, but I was glad to help."

"In return for getting the exclusive on the story when it broke," Mark said.

"I had to get something out of it, too. After I left the paper and started writing books about serial-killer cases full-time,

Lou became one of my principal sources, giving me deep background. It was different then, because he knew what he told me wouldn't see print until the case was closed."

"What was in it for him besides seeing his name in print?" Tanis asked.

"Once my books became bestsellers, I started to get letters and phone calls from killers who wanted me to write about them," Freddy said, absently scratching his arm again. "A few of them didn't wait until they were arrested to start asking. I took the letters in to Lou; I let him tap my phones. The information became invaluable in working up profiles of the killers. I helped him catch a lot of very nasty people."

"And he helped you become rich," Tanis said. "In fact, he's still helping."

Mark gave Tanis a bewildered look.

"Haven't you heard?" Tanis asked. "Freddy already has a million-dollar deal to write a book about Lou Rozan."

Mark was stunned. "That was fast."

"My publisher knew that Lou was my friend and that I've written about every killer he hid behind and that we were working together on this task force when his secret was exposed," Freddy said defensively. "Is there something wrong with that?"

"The body isn't even cold, Freddy," Tanis said.

"This is what I do. I write about serial killers, the cops who pursue them and the people whose lives are forever changed by the experience," Freddy replied. "Only this time, I'm telling my story instead of someone else's. Can you think of a better person to write about it?"

"Or profit from it," Tanis said.

"That's a cheap shot," Freddy said. "You haven't read my books, but Mark has. He can tell you. I'm not a hack."

"You know I'm an admirer of your books," Mark said. "But it does seem like you're capitalizing on your involvement rather quickly."

"If I don't do it, someone else will. And let's face it, wouldn't you rather have me write about it than an outsider who didn't know Lou the way I did?" Freddy said. "This is going to be a serious work that is going to tell the whole story from every perspective. Which means I'm going to need your help."

"Why me?" Mark asked.

"Without you, we would never have known about the killings," Freddy said.

"You are the beginning of the story. I'd like to interview you about everything while the details and the emotions are still fresh in your mind."

That was the problem. It was too fresh. Mark was physically and emotionally exhausted. He hadn't slept for over twenty-four hours. The prospect of going through it all again so soon, if only just to talk about it, was not something he looked forward to. But he could see how writing the book would be a therapeutic experience for Freddy, a way to sort through the feelings of shock and betrayal he was undoubtedly experiencing. And Freddy was right; he was the best person to write about the case. His book could become the first real step towards understanding what had transformed Lou Rozan into a murderer.

"Let me think about it," Mark said, rising from his seat. "I'll get back to you after I've had some rest."

"Fair enough," Freddy said.

Mark glanced at Tanis. "I actually came down here to check on you. Is everything okay?"

"Better than I expected."

"What were you expecting?"

"To be filling out a job application."

Mark motioned to the stacks of dusty file

boxes stacked haphazardly all around them. "You don't mind being back down here in the basement?"

"I'd rather be eating Big Macs than serving them," she replied.

CHAPTER TWENTY

The days that followed Stanley Tidewell's murder were difficult for Dr. Jack Stewart. He couldn't go back to Colorado, not with the Tidewell situation unresolved and the threat of a thirty million dollar lawsuit hanging over his head. It would look too much like he was running away.

He talked regularly to his office in Denver, checked up on his patients and dealt with business, but at best that only took up a couple hours each day. That left him with hours to kill, waiting for a call from Mark either with a task for him to do or with the news that the mystery had been solved.

But the only call he got was the one asking him to participate in the restaging of the transplant operation. During the reenactment, Jack tried to concentrate on his work while at the same time watching everybody else, including Mark and Amanda, who prowled around the room, studying everything. When the operation was over, Mark asked them all to go, re-maining alone in the surgical suites as they were cleaned.

Jack figured Mark was going for authen-ticity. None of them had been in the oper-ating room during the cleanup before, so he didn't want them around now.

Afterwards, Jack waited anxiously for some news, but Mark had been strangely silent, sharing none of his thoughts. It wasn't like it used to be, when Jack was part of the team.

Then again, it wasn't like the Tidewell case was the only thing on Mark's mind. Jack knew Mark was preoccupied with rapid developments in the Silent Partner investigation. But even so, he still felt ex-cluded. If Mark was working on a theory, he wasn't sharing it with him.

To distract himself and eat up the empty hours, Jack tried watching sports, reading cheap paperbacks and going to movies, but he couldn't concentrate; his mind kept wandering back to the transplant operation and his uncertain future. So he spent more and more time in the hotel gym, exercising to occupy himself and work off his mounting anxiety.

Most evenings, Jack inevitably ended up at BBQ Bob's, having dinner and talking long into the night with Jesse, who seemed to be as out of the loop on the Tidewell case as he was.

Or was he?

Although Jack found himself liking Jesse more with each day, he couldn't help wondering if his newfound friend knew more than he was telling, which was zilch. Jack even pressed Susan for information but without success. While Jesse seemed to warm up to Jack, Susan remained cold, almost hostile. Jack didn't know whether it was because he was taking up so much of Jesse's time, or if she knew something she wasn't telling.

Jack kept his distance from Amanda, because he knew if they spent any time alone together, she'd want to talk more about why he left. With all the other problems in his life right now, that was the last thing Jack wanted to deal with. Still, he felt guilty about missing the opportunity to get to know her again and to meet her son. He told himself there would be plenty of time to make amends once the Tidewell situation was resolved. Unless resolution meant losing his medical license and every cent that he had.

The morning after the Silent Partner press conference, he resisted the urge to call or visit Mark. Instead, Jack went to BBQ Bob's for breakfast on the off-chance that Mark or Steve might come in for a bite.

He found Amanda and Jesse there, on opposite sides of the counter, talking over cups of coffee. Jack slid onto the stool beside Amanda and the three of them discussed the Silent Partner case for a while over their breakfasts, just like everybody else in the city was doing that morning.

"How are you holding up?" Amanda asked.

"Fine," Jack replied.

Amanda glanced at Jesse. "How about you?"

"Fine," Jesse replied, refilling their coffees.

Amanda added about two cups of sugar to her cup of coffee and stirred. "You're not worried about how the Tidewell situation is going to shake out."

"Mark's on it," Jesse said. "That's good enough for me."

"Me, too," Jack said.

Amanda studied them skeptically over the rim of her cup as she sipped her thick brew. "Really?"

"Why?" Jack asked. "Do you know something we don't?"

"I'm as much in the dark as you are," Amanda replied.

"Does this mean that Mark is stumped?" Jack asked. "Or does he know something that we don't?"

"If he knows something," Jesse said, "he's keeping it to himself."

"Why would he do that?" Jack asked.

"Maybe he doesn't trust us anymore," Jesse said.

"Maybe he thinks one of us is guilty," Jack said.

"You think so?" Jesse asked.

"Do you?" Jack asked.

Amanda smiled to herself. Jack and Jesse both stared at her.

"What's so damn funny?" Jesse asked.

"Nothing," Amanda said, taking another sip of coffee. "I'm just relieved neither one of you is getting too stressed out."

Jesse went back into the kitchen, leaving Amanda and Jack to themselves. Jack moved the food around his plate with his fork, Amanda watching him out of the corner of her eye.

"If you were my son," Amanda said, "I'd tell you to stop playing with your food."

Jack nodded and continued to rearrange his bacon strips.

She snatched the fork from his hand.

"You want to talk about what's bothering you?"

"No." Jack stuck a spoon in his coffee and started stirring it instead.

Amanda watched him for a moment, then took the cup away from him.

"Too bad," she said. "Talk."

Jack glanced at her, then found something fascinating about his napkin to look at.

"I didn't really leave Community General for the money," Jack said. "The years I spent here, with you and Mark and Steve, it was the best, worth far more than any paycheck. Practicing medicine, helping Mark solve murders — it was great. The happiest time of my life. Nothing will ever compare to that."

"Then why leave it behind?" Amanda said. "You didn't have to go."

"You drove me to it."

"Me?" she asked defensively. "What did I do?"

"You were beautiful, smart and fearless," Jack said, folding and refolding his napkin. "You were game for any challenge, though you could be a real pain in the ass about it. Boy, how you liked to argue. Still, you were always there for me, supporting me no matter what. You were like the sister I always wanted and never had."

"Was there something wrong with that?" she asked, yanking the napkin away from him.

"Not until I fell in love with you."

Amanda was too shocked to speak. She simply froze, staring at him. How could she not have known?

But if she was honest with herself, and she usually was, Amanda realized she knew all along; she just never dared face it before. Wasn't that attraction, that flirtation, the real spark behind all their arguing and teasing? It wasn't an accident that they always found a reason to go off together on their investigations for Mark. In fact, wasn't that half the reason they were helping Mark in the first place? If she didn't know Jack loved her, why did it hurt so much and for so long when he left?

"I knew you didn't feel the same way about me," Jack said gently. "It got so every minute I spent around you was torture. I tried to ignore my feelings by dating every woman that came along, but it only made things worse. Finally, I couldn't take it any more. I had to go."

"Why didn't you tell me?" Amanda asked, her voice barely a whisper.

"Because it would have been wrong. You

were like my sister," Jack said. "If I'd told you then, it would have ruined everything between us."

"So you just ran away," Amanda said, not even trying to disguise the hurt in her voice.

Jack nodded and looked down at his feet. They were both silent for a moment.

"Do you still love me?" Amanda asked tentatively.

"Yes." Jack looked up and smiled warmly. "But like a brother."

Amanda held out her arms to him. They embraced, holding each other tightly.

"Oh, Jack," she whispered, "you're such an idiot."

Jack smiled. "It's good to know your feelings for me haven't changed."

Mark slept in until nearly eleven that morning. It was a deep, dreamless sleep. He awoke feeling completely refreshed, which only made him aware of how much tension he'd actually been carrying over the last few days. But now he felt like himself again, full of energy, his mind clear and sharp.

He took a long hot shower, dressed in casual clothes and padded barefoot into the kitchen, opening the refrigerator to see if there was something special he could make himself for breakfast.

Mark browsed through the refrigerator, checking out the leftover pizza, barbecue ribs and Chinese food. He sniffed the thick-sliced bacon, smoked salmon, kosher salami and all the cheeses. He examined the fresh melons, table grapes and navel oranges. He sorted through all the different varieties of yogurt. He even reorganized the milk, juices, beer and soft drinks.

He did everything except actually decide on something to eat. There was just too much to choose from. Or was the problem something else?

The phone rang, distracting him from his quandary. Mark closed the refrigerator and grabbed the phone. It was Clarke Trotter, the Community General attorney, inviting Mark to a settlement conference that afternoon with Billy Tidewell.

Mark promised to be there and told Trotter to invite Jack and Jesse as well. Trotter argued that their lawsuits were a separate matter and that including them in the proceedings could hurt Community General's negotiating position. But Mark argued the opposite, insisting that their presence was essential to the hospital winning an acceptable settlement.

Trotter pressed for specifics, but Mark refused, saying it would all come out in the meeting. The attorney reluctantly gave in. Mark hung up the phone, settled for an apple from the fruit bowl on the counter and started searching for his shoes.

Billy Tidewell, face rigid with anger, sat on one side of the vast conference table with his lawyer, Sandra Shelling, a crisp young woman in a crisp suit looking crisply at Clarke Trotter and the three doctors across from her.

"I don't think the facts of this case are in dispute," Shelling said. "Stanley Tidewell was admitted for a routine kidney transplant and was killed due to the gross incompetence of your doctors."

"What happened to Mr. Tidewell was a horrible tragedy," Trotter said. "The staff of Community General Hospital was as shocked and saddened by his death as anyone else."

"Not as much as me," Billy Tidewell said, his voice even and measured as he tried to control his anger. "This operation was supposed to save my father's life, not take it from him."

"Of course we agree with you," Trotter said, "and you have our deepest sympathy."

"That's not enough," Shelling said.

"The thrust of your argument is that his death was the fault of our doctors," Trotter said. "But the fact is, the only Community General surgeon involved was Dr. Travis, who operated on you, Mr. Tidewell. That aspect of the operation proceeded smoothly, as you can attest. The fatal error, if one was made, occurred during the implantation of the organ at the hands of an outside doctor your father flew in from another state."

Jack stiffened in his seat. So this was how it was going down. He couldn't blame Community General for making him take the fall for everyone, but he was surprised, and deeply hurt, that Mark was going along with it. He glanced at Mark, who refused to meet his gaze.

Jesse could see where this was going, too. Although the argument Trotter was presenting was to Jesse's benefit, it still astonished him that Mark wasn't putting up a fight on Jack's behalf. He wondered what leverage Community General used against Mark to assure his cooperation. Or maybe Mark simply agreed with what Trotter was saying. Which meant that Mark must have discovered that Jack *was* responsible for Stanley Tidewell's death.

"Oh, in that case, never mind." Shelling made a show of gathering up her documents, then smirked at Trotter. "Do you really believe that just because Stanley Tidewell brought in an outside doctor, the hospital is absolved of any responsibility for what happened? I don't think a judge or jury will see it that way."

"My point, Ms. Shelling, is that our alleged culpability in this matter is significantly less than Dr. Stewart's; therefore the monetary compensation you're seeking from us should reflect that reality," Trotter said. "I think we can arrive at a far more reasonable, and less substantial, figure that will spare Mr. Tidewell, and Community General, a protracted and unpleasant legal proceeding. We think one million dollars is a fair settlement for all concerned."

"You're every bit as guilty as he is," Billy said, pointing an accusing finger at Jack. "Nobody stopped him from giving my father an antibiotic that any competent doctor should have known would kill him."

"The antibiotic didn't kill him," Mark said.

"How do you know that?" Shelling asked.

"Because I gave Stanley the same antibiotic several months ago and he survived."

Trotter groaned before he could catch himself. Billy Tidewell and Sandra Shelling stared at Mark in dismay. Jesse and Jack were shocked, too, for much the same reason that Trotter was. How could Mark have so blithely admitted something like that? Didn't he realize what he was doing to himself and the hospital?

"I think that pretty much torpedoes your argument, Mr. Trotter," Shelling said, making a notation on her legal pad. "I don't know what is more chilling here, the rampant incompetence of your doctors or their arrogance."

"Aren't you curious about how he died?" Mark asked. "Or is it just about the money?"

"He died of anaphylactic shock," Billy said. "Because somebody didn't realize he was allergic to penicillin."

"Actually, the opposite is true," Mark said. "He was killed by someone who knew exactly what Stanley was allergic to."

"You're admitting that he was killed by an allergic reaction to penicillin and that it wasn't accidental?" Shelling asked Mark incredulously.

"Of course," Mark said. "Isn't it obvious?"

Trotter cleared his throat. "I think it

would be best, Dr. Sloan, if you allowed me to do the talking."

"Not if you intend to pay them a penny for something this hospital is not responsible for," Mark said.

"Are you denying that Stanley Tidewell was killed in your operating room while undergoing kidney transplant surgery?" Shelling asked.

"No, that's exactly what happened," Mark said.

"You're not making any sense!" Trotter shouted, momentarily losing control of his anger.

Jack and Jesse shared a look. The truth was, they weren't following Mark's reasoning any better than Trotter was, but they knew something he didn't. They recognized that sparkle in Mark's eyes, the grin playing at the corners of his mouth. The two young doctors didn't know how Mark was getting there, but they knew where he was going. He'd solved the mystery.

"Stanley Tidewell was murdered," Mark said. "And it happened in plain sight during the operation."

"You're saying the doctors and nurses stood there and did nothing while my father was killed?" Billy said, red-faced with rage.

"Yes," Mark said.

Trotter covered his face with his hands. He was certain now of two things: The hospital was going to lose tens of millions of dollars, and Dr. Sloan was insane.

"To be fair, though, they were all unwilling accomplices," Mark said.

"I don't see how that's possible," Shelling said.

"That's exactly what the murderer intended," Mark said. "There was no way anyone in that operating room could have tainted the kidney with penicillin, accidentally or intentionally, without exposing himself as the killer. So there's only one possible explanation." Mark glanced at Billy. "Would you like to tell us?"

"It's obvious," Billy said. "Everyone in the operating room knows who is responsible and they're covering up for each other."

"There's a much simpler explanation," Mark said. "The kidney was tainted *before* the operation."

"That's impossible," Shelling said. "The kidney was inside Billy until the moment that Dr. Travis —"

She stopped herself, realizing too late what she was saying.

"Once I realized how the murder was committed, all that was left was finding a

301

motive." Mark looked Billy Tidewell in the eye. "Then I remembered how interested you were right before the operation in the UCLA game. So much so that you asked the doctors to record it for you. The game was also the first thing you asked me about after the operation. Not how your father was. Or even how you were. So I had my son talk to some bookies around town. You've got quite a gambling problem, Billy."

"That's got nothing to do with what this hospital did to my father," Billy said. "This is a pathetic attempt to smear the victim to save yourselves."

"You were in enormous debt, all of which could be easily wiped away if you had your father's fortune," Mark said. "The stumbling block was that your father had to die first. So you talked him into the kidney transplant. You figured if you donated your kidney to save your father's life, nobody would ever suspect you of killing him, of using your own kidney as a murder weapon."

"I don't need to sit here and listen to any more of this." Billy got up and opened the door, to find Steve Sloan and two uniformed police officers waiting in the hallway.

"I always love this part," Jesse said to Jack. "Don't you?"

"What's going on here?" Shelling asked.

"I hope you've got some experience in criminal law," Steve said to Shelling, flashing his badge. "Your client is under arrest for the murder of Stanley Tidewell."

Steve read him his rights. Billy began to laugh.

"This is a joke, right? You're saying I killed my own father with my kidney?"

"Billy, I strongly advise you not to say another word," Shelling said.

"It's all just talk, Sandra," Billy said, motioning to Mark. "They don't have any proof."

"Actually, we do," Mark said. "You had a blood test the morning of the surgery. I had it analyzed again and found traces of penicillin."

Billy's smile faded and he lowered his head. He began to sob. When he raised his face again, tears were rolling down his cheeks.

"I woke up that morning with a sore throat. I was afraid you'd cancel the operation if I told you, so I took a pen tab." His chin quivered. "I had no idea my father was allergic to penicillin. . . . I didn't know until after he was dead, after they told me

303

how he died. I've got to live with that guilt for the rest of my life."

Now it was Sandra Shelling's turn to groan. Her client had just admitted to falsely accusing the hospital and two doctors of malpractice and to his own culpability in his father's death. Trotter, on the other hand, had brightened up considerably.

"That's a very good story, Billy," Mark said, nodding appreciatively. "You might even have wriggled free with it, if only there wasn't five grams of penicillin in your system. That's ten times the usual dosage. Hard to see that as anything but an intentional overdose. Harmless to you, but deadly for your dad. You wanted to be absolutely certain there was enough penicillin in your kidney to kill him."

Billy wiped the crocodile tears from his cheeks and glared at Mark with pure hatred. "You know how many times I asked my father for a loan? He told me it was my problem. To deal with it like a man. He would have let them break my legs rather than part with a goddamn penny of our money. He'd do that to his own flesh and blood. So it's only appropriate that his own flesh and blood is what killed him, don't you think?"

"Billy, shut up," Shelling said, then turned to Steve. "We're finished here."

"You certainly are," Jack said with a grin.

Steve handcuffed Billy and led him away. Sandra Shelling gathered up her papers and followed after him.

Trotter gave Mark a big smile. "I don't know what to say, Dr. Sloan."

"You could start by apologizing to Jack," Mark said.

"Don't bother," Jack said, clapping Trotter on the back and grinning mischievously. "I think I'd rather sue."

CHAPTER TWENTY-ONE

Everyone gathered at Mark's beach house that night to celebrate the conclusion of the Tidewell case. Jesse and Steve supplied heaping plates of hickory-smoked spareribs, fresh corn bread and slow-baked beans from BBQ Bob's. Amanda brought over an enormous cake and Susan whipped up some Hawaiian-style tropical drinks.

Since Amanda and Susan hadn't been part of the settlement conference and the arrest of Billy Tidewell, they insisted over dinner that Mark and Jack tell them everything that happened, leaving nothing out.

Mark gladly went over the clues in the case and the deductions he made that led him to suspect, and ultimately expose, Billy Tidewell's guilt. Jack added his own play-by-play, even admitting that he thought Mark was betraying him until he saw the telltale sparkle in the doctor's eyes.

"I forgot just how much fun it is watching you in action," Jack said to Mark. "Of course, it's a lot more fun when it isn't my neck on the line."

"You were never in this alone, Jack," Mark said. "The reputations of every doctor and nurse at Community General were also at stake."

"There's one thing I don't get," Jesse said. "How could Billy possibly have known that Jack would prescribe cephalosporin as a pre-op antibiotic?"

"He didn't," Mark said. "Billy just got lucky. I think Billy's plan was to point suspicion at you, Jesse, by convincing his dad to open a Burger Beach right across the street from your restaurant."

"Which would give me a strong motive for killing him and for you to cover up for me," Jesse said, "considering you're our largest investor."

"Not to mention our *only* investor," Steve added.

"Speaking of money," Amanda said, looking at Jack. "You aren't really going to sue the hospital, are you?"

"No," Jack replied, "but think I'll let Trotter sweat for a while."

"It will be good for him," Jesse said. "Maybe he'll burn off some of that beer belly."

Susan nudged Jesse playfully. "You're terrible."

"What do you mean? I'm just concerned about his health," Jesse said. "I'm a doctor who never stops caring."

Amanda turned to Jack. "So, I guess you'll be heading back to Denver right away."

"Actually, I'm staying in town for the weekend."

"Meet someone interesting?" she asked, teasingly.

"As a matter of fact, I did," Jack said.

Steve shook his head in amused disbelief. "You haven't changed a bit."

"Is she anybody we know?" Susan asked.

"I think so," Jack said to her. "She's an amazing woman with boundless energy. She's raising a kid on her own and juggling two jobs, one at the hospital and one at the medical examiner's office."

"Jack . . ." Amanda began, embarrassed.

"I'd like to get to know her again and find out all the things in her life that I've missed," Jack said, continuing to direct his comments to Susan. "Most of all, I'm looking forward to meeting her son. If he's anything like his mom, he must be a great kid. I was thinking of taking them both to Disneyland. Think they'll go for it?"

"On one condition," Amanda said, trying hard to sound strong and forceful.

Jack turned to her. "What?"

"You start behaving like a member of this family again," Amanda said. "We want phone calls, letters, e-mails and regular visits."

"An invitation to visit you in Colorado wouldn't hurt," Steve said. "Particularly during ski season."

Jack gave him a look. Steve shrugged innocently.

"What Steve is trying to say is that we all missed you," Mark said.

"I didn't," Jesse piped in. Susan gave him another nudge, only this one wasn't playful or gentle. He grabbed his side in pain.

Jack smiled and offered Amanda his hand. "You got a deal."

She reached for his hand but instead of shaking it, pulled him into a hug.

"Hey." Jesse tapped Jack on the shoulder. "When we come to Colorado, will you let me drive your SL?"

Jesse dodged another attack from Susan and everybody laughed, Jack harder than anybody, glad to be rescued just when things were getting too emotional for his comfort.

But Mark basked in the warmth that comes only from family and the shared joy that comes when good friends and family are brought together. They spent the next few hours sharing stories, laughing, teasing and remembering good times. It felt to Mark like all the holidays rolled into one long evening. He promised himself that he'd find a way to do this more often, that he wouldn't wait until days that came with their own line of greeting cards.

But as much as he didn't want the night to end, responsibilities intruded. Amanda had a babysitter who had to get home. Jesse and Susan needed some sleep before their shifts at the hospital. And Steve was exhausted, the sleepless hours he spent on the Silent Partner case suddenly catching up with him all at once.

So while Steve cleaned up, Mark saw their guests out. Jack was the last to go. Jack hesitated at the door, not sure how to say what he wanted to say. Finally, he just shrugged and offered Mark his hand.

"Thank you, Mark," Jack said. "For everything."

"Our door is always open," Mark smiled warmly. "I want you to think of this as your home."

"I do," Jack said.

Mark watched Jack go, then closed the door and went to the kitchen, where Steve was trying to fit all the leftovers into the already overstuffed refrigerator.

"We should have had Jesse and Amanda take some of this with them," Steve said. "What are we going to do with all this food?"

"You could take it downstairs to your kitchen," Mark suggested, knowing full well that was what Steve wanted all along.

"If you insist," Steve whined unconvincingly, his back to Mark as he picked up the cake, a victorious smile on his face.

Mark started to rearrange food on the shelves to create some room, when he looked down at the plate of ribs in one hand and the carton of milk in the other and had a very strange feeling, like a mental hot flash. Now he knew why he'd stood in front of the refrigerator that morning, unable to choose something for breakfast. His mind was trying to tell him something.

But what?

"Wait," Mark said.

Steve stopped, his shoulders sagging. "I almost made a clean getaway." He turned, bringing the cake back to the table. "Okay, I'll leave you half the cake and, in return, I'll take the potato salad off your hands."

That's when Steve saw his father frozen in place, still holding the ribs and the milk, staring into the refrigerator as if it was a doorway opening into another dimension.

"Dad?" Steve asked, suddenly very concerned. "Are you feeling all right?"

"I'm feeling fine." Mark turned around and gave Steve the stuff in his hands. "Take this."

Then Mark turned back to the refrigerator and handed Steve a jar of pickles and a half-empty bottle of spaghetti sauce. "And this."

But Mark didn't stop there. He passed Steve the fruit, the cheese, the vegetables, the cold cuts, the juice, the soft drinks, the bacon, the pudding, the leftover pizza, the eggs, the Chinese food, the yogurt, the potato salad and every other item on every shelf until the refrigerator and the freezer were empty, and the kitchen table and counters were overflowing with food.

Mark closed the refrigerator, crossed his arms under his chest and studied everything on the table and counters.

"Dad, what are you doing?" Steve asked. "Just throw out the stuff that's rotten, keep what you want and we'll put the rest in my fridge. It's not that complicated."

"Not for us, it isn't," Mark said, still studying the food. "We can eat whatever we want."

Steve glanced at the food, then at his dad. "Yeah, so?"

Mark looked up at Steve. "I thought the Silent Partner broke his pattern when he tried to kill me, but he didn't."

"Wait a minute." Steve shook his head in confusion. "What do our leftovers have to do with the Silent Partner?"

"He always made his killings look like the work of someone else," Mark said. "He did the same thing with his last victim."

"But we don't know who his last victim was yet."

"Yes, we do," Mark said. "It was Lou Rozan."

Mark sat in silence, lost in his thoughts, as Steve drove them to Rozan's place, taking the winding canyon road from Malibu through the Santa Monica Mountains and down into the San Fernando Valley.

Traffic was light at that time of night, and since Mark didn't feel like talking, Steve kept himself occupied by trying to second-guess what was going through his father's mind.

It was futile, of course, and Steve knew it. His mind just wasn't wired like his father's. It was times like this that forced

Steve to confront the uncomfortable truth about himself. While he was a diligent, hardworking detective, it was basically a learned skill, honed through years of trial and error. He had no natural affinity for it.

But with his father, it was different. Anything could trigger that instant of absolute clarity when thousands of unrelated facts came together into an obvious solution.

Mark Sloan's astonishing acuity was a gift, one that Steve knew he didn't share. Steve knew he could never look at a messy refrigerator and see anything but a messy refrigerator.

So, since he couldn't decipher what the food in their refrigerator meant, all Steve had to work with was what his father had said, which didn't make a lot of sense.

Steve knew his father didn't mean to talk in riddles, but when Mark's synapses were firing that fast, that was invariably how the words came out.

The last person the Silent Partner killed was himself, at least that's what Steve assumed. So how did the food in their refrigerator change anything?

Steve wasn't any closer to the answer when he pulled up in front of Lou Rozan's house. The entire property was still illuminated by the floodlights. A uniformed police officer sat in a squad car that had been positioned to block the gap in the rose-covered fence. His partner covered the driveway gate, sitting on a folding chair beside the wrecked Honda.

The Sloans got out of the car and approached the gate. Steve flashed his badge at the officer, who let them in.

The house was eerily quiet. Even though the property was bathed in the harsh light, there was still something dark and foreboding about the house.

Steve cut the yellow crime-scene tape, opened the door for his father and then followed him inside.

The house had the rancid, sour odor of death and decay. It was dark inside, but neither one of them turned on the lights. They didn't want, or need, to see the blood splatter on the walls or the large stains on the chair where Lou's corpse once sat.

Mark pulled out a Mini Maglite, using the narrow beam to make his way into the kitchen. He went straight for the refrigerator, opening the door and illuminating himself in the arc of light cast by the interior bulb.

He motioned Steve over and stepped aside, holding the door open for him. "Take a look inside and tell me what you see."

Steve leaned in. "A couple bottles of wine, some apples, oranges and melons, a nice pineapple, carrots, a jar of pickles, some cartons of juice and two six-packs of diet root beer."

Mark opened the freezer. "And here?"

"Popsicles, frozen orange juice and some crusty old ice cubes," he said.

"What don't you see?"

"A mess," Steve said. "Did you drag me out here just to show me how neat and orderly Lou's refrigerator is?"

"I don't see any steaks or hamburger, pork or chicken, do you?"

"So he was a vegetarian," Steve said.

"There's also no milk, eggs or fish. No pudding, cake, tofu or yogurt. No cream cheese, butter or chocolate syrup," Mark said. "There's no ice cream or frozen pizzas in the freezer, either."

"I don't see what you're getting at."

"People have all kinds of food in their refrigerators, but Lou didn't. Not even one leftover or restaurant doggie bag," Mark said. "That's not normal. I haven't opened the pantry yet, but I'm certain you won't find any nuts or cereal, bread or rice, chips or pasta."

"So he was a healthy eater," Steve said, yawning. "Dad, it's after midnight, I'm bushed and I really don't see what you're getting at here."

"I think Lou Rozan suffered from mild phenylketonuria," Mark said. "It's a genetic disorder that disrupts the body's ability to metabolize an amino acid called phenylalanine, which is found in nearly all foods that contain protein. If phenylalanine builds up in the body, it can cause serious brain damage and seizures."

"You can tell Rozan had the disorder just from the food in his refrigerator?"

"And also by the food he brought for lunch each day while we were on the task force," Mark said. "But there's more. The disorder also interferes with the body's ability to produce tyrosine, an amino acid that's a necessary component of melanin, which gives hair and skin its coloring."

"That's why Lou Rozan had blond hair, blue eyes and a light complexion," Steve said, following the logic. "But even if Rozan had phenyl-whatever, what difference does that make now?"

Mark pulled out a bottle of the Oakes Diet Root Beer from the refrigerator and held it out to Steve. "Read the warning label."

" 'Attention, Phenylketonurics: This beverage contains phenylalanine,' " Steve read. "I've always wondered what that meant."

"The artificial sweetener aspartame is loaded with phenylalanine," Mark said. "Lou Rozan would never drink this. No one with his disorder would."

"He didn't have to drink the root beer to leave the bottle cap at crime scenes."

"That's true," Mark said. "So ask yourself, why would he bother to refrigerate it?"

"He wouldn't." Steve slammed the refrigerator door shut in frustration. He looked his father in the eye. "The Silent Partner is still out there, isn't he?"

Mark nodded gravely. "He murdered Lou Rozan and made it look like Lou killed himself."

"Laying the blame for his killing on someone else, just like all his other victims," Steve said. "The clever bastard repeated his pattern again."

"And he will keep repeating it until he's stopped," Mark said, his voice cold with grim certainty.

Dawn in the morgue is no way to start a day, Steve thought to himself, as he sat in an uncomfortable chair, nursing a lukewarm cup of lousy coffee and waiting for

Amanda to return with the lab results. Mark sat beside him, reading Amanda's autopsy report on Lou Rozan.

"How did the killer get into Lou's house?" Steve asked. "The place was like a fortress."

Mark closed the file and looked up at Steve. "I think he was invited in. That's why the Honda was parked in the driveway and the alarm was off when we arrived."

"Then the killer is someone Lou knew and trusted."

"It could be someone *we* know and trust," Mark said.

Steve pondered that unsettling thought for a moment. Tanis Archer, Terry Riordan and Chief Masters all worked cases that the Silent Partner copied. And they all knew Rozan well enough to get invited into his house. But whether it was one of them or not, what happened after the killer got inside?

"Lou definitely pulled the trigger. There was only one bullet fired from that gun, and there was gunpowder residue on Lou's hand and sleeve," Steve said. "He wouldn't have done it without putting up a fight. But there were no signs of a struggle. The room was clean, nothing was broken and there were no bruises or defensive wounds on Lou's body."

"That's because he couldn't fight back."

"Why not?"

"The answer is in the autopsy report," Mark said, tapping the file. "The killer knew Lou well enough to know he was on Xanax. My guess is the killer either spiked Lou's wine with the drug without his knowledge or forced him at gunpoint to take an overdose. Either way, all the killer had to do was wait until the drugs kicked in and Lou was defenseless, put the gun in his hand, and pull the trigger."

"Neat and simple," Steve said, shaking his head in disgust. "Then he just climbed the fence and walked away, his frame-up complete."

Mark gave Steve a curious look. "I hadn't thought of that. . . ." he said, his voice trailing off.

"Thought of what?" Steve asked.

That's when Amanda strode in, stifling a yawn as she flipped through a sheaf of papers. "You were right, Mark. We checked Rozan's DNA and his blood. He definitely had mild phenylketonuria."

"Thanks, Amanda; we needed to be sure," Mark said. "I hope we didn't ruin your Disneyland plans."

"No, we can still make it. Jack isn't

coming to pick us up until nine," Amanda said. "Though I might end up sleeping through Pirates of the Caribbean. Is there anything more I can do to help?"

"Not unless you'd like to call and wake up the chief for me," Steve said.

"No, thanks," Amanda said. "I think I'd rather stake myself to an anthill."

Steve groaned and rose from his seat, taking out his cell phone. "He isn't going to like this."

"Wait a minute before you make that call," Mark said. "I think I may know how to soften the blow."

CHAPTER TWENTY-TWO

While Steve talked, Chief Masters stood at his window, looking out at the city like a king surveying his kingdom. Agent Riordan kept shifting in his seat, unable to get comfortable, his face tight.

When Steve finished, Terry couldn't sit still any longer. He got up out of his chair and started pacing around the chief's huge office.

"This is a disaster," Terry said.

"That's one way of looking at it," Steve said. "I like to think we've narrowly avoided one."

"How can you say that?" Terry asked.

"We believed that Lou Rozan was guilty and that he committed suicide. If Dad hadn't figured out that we were tricked, then as soon as the case was closed and the task force was disbanded, the Silent Partner would have started killing again."

"You're missing the big picture, Detective," the chief said, turning around. "Two days ago, we disclosed that both the LAPD and the FBI bungled the investigations of at least half a dozen serial-killer cases that we know of, putting all those convictions in serious jeopardy. We also disclosed that, as a result, another serial killer got to run around the state murdering people without us even noticing. And if that wasn't bad enough, we disclosed that the killer got away with it because he was an FBI profiler we counted on to help us identify and capture serial killers. It would have been hard enough for either the LAPD or the FBI to emerge from that controversy and still retain the public's confidence and respect. Now it turns out we identified the wrong person as the killer."

"The way I see it, sir, things just got better," Steve said.

"Oh, really, Detective?" the chief said. "How so?"

"We're rehabilitating the reputation of a respected profiler and showing the public that the killer couldn't outsmart us."

"It's too late for that," Terry snapped. "The public knows he's outsmarted us. Now we're just going to look like fools."

"But we didn't fall for his trick," Steve argued.

"That might be how we present it, but it's not how the media will report it or how the public will perceive it," the chief said. "We held a press conference and declared that Lou Rozan was the killer. We were wrong. That is the bottom line. That is what will be remembered. Even when we catch the killer, and we *will*, we'll have a hard time convincing the public that we are right this time. It's going to be an even harder sell to a judge and jury."

"We have to bury this for as long as we can," Terry said.

"I agree," the chief said. "If possible, I'd like to delay the disclosure until we can announce that we've got the actual killer in custody."

Steve rose from his chair, dismayed at what he was hearing. "We're talking about an FBI profiler who lost his life in the line of duty. We have to clear his name. We owe him that."

"He's dead," Terry said. "Believe me, he won't mind."

"He has a family that thinks he was a serial killer," Steve said. "Do you have any idea what they must be going through?"

"I sympathize with their pain, Detective," the chief said, "but this isn't just about public perception. It's about the integrity of an ongoing investigation. It's to our benefit to have the killer believe for as long as possible that we fell for his deception."

"He already knows we didn't," Steve said. "And if he doesn't, he will before the day is out."

"How can you possibly know that?" Terry said.

"Because we were right about one thing," Steve said. "The killer is one of us."

The chief glanced at Terry, then back at Steve, giving him a long, appraising look. "Assuming you're right, Detective, what do you suggest?"

"I don't have any suggestions," Steve said. "But my dad has a pretty good one."

Mark was in such a hurry to act on his hunch the previous night that he'd forgotten about the food he'd emptied out of the refrigerator. He was reminded of it the instant he returned home the next morning and was assaulted by the rotting odor of spoiled food.

He changed into a pair of old hospital scrubs, put on a pair of rubber gloves and a surgical mask and got to work cleaning up. He stuffed everything into an enormous trash bag, which he lugged to the garbage cans outside. Then he came back in, opened up the windows to air out the house and spent the next hour scrubbing the counters and mopping the floor.

Mark was just finishing up when the doorbell rang. He peeled off his rubber gloves and went to answer the door. Freddy Meeks was standing there, his hair a mess, his wrinkled shirt untucked from his jeans, a sheepish grin on his face.

"Did I interrupt you in the middle of an operation?" Freddy asked.

Mark laughed self-consciously and pulled down his surgical mask. "Oh, sorry. I was doing some housecleaning. Come on in."

He stepped aside and let Freddy in. "I've got some fresh coffee brewing if you'd like some."

"Great," Freddy said, following Mark to the kitchen. Mark offered him a seat at the table by the window and went to serve the coffee.

"So, what brings you by, Freddy?" Mark asked from the kitchen.

"Would you believe I came by to autograph all my books for you?"

"I don't think so."

Freddy scratched his arm and glanced out at the spectacular ocean view. "It's about my book on the Silent Partner."

Mark came in, set a cup and a bowl of sugar down in front of Freddy and took a seat across from him. "I'm afraid I'm out of cream."

"That's fine; I take it black."

"I'm sorry I haven't had a chance to get back to you about the interview," Mark said. "I was tied up negotiating the settlement of a lawsuit against the hospital."

"You can relax, Mark. I didn't come here to nag you about that. I had plenty of other interviews set up to keep me busy for a while." Freddy scratched his chest. "The thing is, they've all evaporated. Two days ago everybody wanted to talk about the case. Today, I'm getting totally stonewalled. Nobody's returning my calls and nobody wants to see me."

"So that's why you just stopped by instead of calling."

"Something is definitely going down, Mark. I thought if anybody could tell me what's happening, it's you, and I didn't want to get your answering machine."

Mark took a deep breath and let it out slowly. "I suppose you deserve to know."

"That doesn't sound good."

"There's good news and bad news, but this is strictly off the record. I'm only telling you this because you were Lou's old friend," Mark said. "The good news is that we were wrong. Lou Rozan is not the Silent Partner."

Freddy leaned back in his chair, stunned. "I knew it couldn't be true. Lou was a good man and a great cop. This will be a great relief to his family; I know they've been struggling with this as hard as I have."

Freddy scratched his shoulder and leaned forward again. "Ever since his breakdown, he's had a rough time. Night terrors, insomnia, panic attacks. He used to joke about putting a bullet in his head, but I never took it seriously. Lou wasn't a quitter."

"He didn't kill himself, Freddy. His murder was staged to look like suicide."

"So that's the bad news. The Silent Partner is still on the loose."

Mark nodded, then motioned to Freddy's arm, which he was absently scratching. "You keep scratching. What's wrong?"

Freddy shrugged. "It's nothing, just some poison oak."

"I'm a doctor, you know. Why don't you let me take a look at it?" Mark said, rising from his seat.

"No, it's okay."

"I promise I won't charge you for a house call," Mark said with a smile.

Freddy reluctantly rolled up his sleeve to expose a bumpy red rash on his arm, crisscrossing his skin like tiny whiplashes.

"No wonder you're scratching. The skin is badly inflamed. The itching must be driving you crazy," Mark said. "I've got some cortisone cream in my medical bag that will take care of that."

Mark went into the living room, opened his bag and searched inside for the cream.

"How did you figure it out?" Freddy asked.

"It wasn't a particularly difficult diagnosis to make."

"I meant Lou's suicide. How did you know it was murder?"

Mark found the tube of cream and some cotton and returned to the table.

"To understand that, I have to tell you a little about what we know about the Silent Partner," Mark said, putting some cream on the cotton and gently dabbing it on Freddy's rash. "You already know that he made his killings look like the crimes of others. What you don't know is that he always left a calling card behind. Actually, it was thanks to your book that we made that discovery."

Mark went back into the living room and pulled Freddy's books off the bookshelf and brought them back to the table.

"It was the cover of this one, *Faces of Death*, that tipped me off. It's the picture the killer took of the French tourist. You see that bottle cap beside the body? It's from an Oakes Diet Root Beer. We found one just like it at the scene of every murder the Silent Partner committed."

Freddy looked at the cover, fascinated. "It was right there in front of our faces all the time and we never saw it."

"I think that's why the killer took the picture in the first place," Mark said. "It was his way of making sure we didn't miss it this time. But it still took years. It's a good thing you decided to put that picture on the cover of your book."

"So what does all this have to do with Lou?"

"I'm getting to that," Mark said, going back to dabbing Freddy's rash with cortisone. "The reason the Silent Partner escaped detection for so long was because he was too good at what he did. His killings were always blamed on others. He was the perfect mimic. And he only could have accomplished that with inside information."

"You figured the killer had to be someone working the cases," Freddy said. "That's what pointed you towards Lou."

"Not just someone who worked the cases, but someone who knew we'd discovered the existence of the Silent Partner," Mark said. "But it wasn't until someone tried to gun me down that we knew for sure."

"You've made a lot of enemies; how did you know the attempt on your life had something to do with the Silent Partner?"

"Because we matched the bullets to the same gun that was used to kill the French tourist." Mark finished with Freddy's arm and sat down in his chair again. "The Silent Partner never really intended to kill me that day. He wanted us to find the bullets; he wanted us to know that the gun was back in play so he could use it to set someone else up for the crime. Which brings us to Lou. The killer and Lou were friends."

"Why do you say that?" Freddy asked.

"You've seen Lou's house. It's got everything but a moat and guard towers," Mark said. "The killer was buzzed in. He drove his car through the gate and parked it in the driveway. The car, incidentally, was the stolen Honda the shooter chased me with."

"He was parking it there to frame Lou," Freddy said, tapping his fingers on the table. "The killer didn't want there to be any doubt left in your minds."

"You're putting it together now," Mark said. "The killer came in, maybe with a grocery bag, but I'm just guessing. Lou offered his guest a glass of wine, or the killer brought the bottle with him as a gift, and they opened it up. Either way, at some point in their pleasant conversation, the killer pulled out a gun, the same weapon used to take shots at me and to kill the French tourist. He forced Lou to take an overdose of Xanax and waited until the drugs took effect. Then he put the gun in Lou's hand and made him shoot himself in the head. Then he went into the kitchen, took a couple six-packs of diet root beer out of his grocery bag and put them in the refrigerator."

"That's a frightening scenario," Freddy said.

"It certainly is."

"There's just one thing I don't get," Freddy said, scratching his chest. "What tipped you off that it wasn't a suicide?"

"The Oakes Diet Root Beer," Mark said, meeting Freddy's gaze. "You never should have put it in the refrigerator. That was your mistake."

Freddy's eyes went cold. "My mistake?"

"If you'd put it in the garage or the

pantry, I might never have suspected a thing. But putting it in the fridge — that implied that Lou drank it, and that just wasn't possible. You knew him well, but not well enough to know he had a metabolic disorder that prevented him from drinking aspartame."

"You think I'm the Silent Partner?" Freddy said, his face rigid, all his boyish charm suddenly gone.

"I'm certain of it," Mark said. "You wrote books about every single one of the serial-killer cases that the Silent Partner mimicked. You knew all the details about the serial killings because Lou fed them to you as background for your books. But it wasn't long before you didn't need him as a source; you were talking to the serial killers themselves. Or should I say, they were calling you. But like all serial killers, you couldn't resist leaving your mark. Problem was, nobody noticed it. You even went so far as to take a picture of the bottle cap and hand it to the police, and they still didn't get it."

Mark picked up *Faces of Death* and pointed to the cover. "So, in your frustration, you blew it up and put it on the cover of your book. You must have been thrilled when I finally noticed it."

Freddy leaned forward on the table. "Mark, I know you're desperate to find the killer, to avenge what happened to Lou, which is the only reason I'm not going to take this personally. Just listen to what you're saying. Be reasonable. There's no evidence."

"Sure, there is," Mark said, motioning to Freddy's arm. "It's all over you. Your rash is from climbing over Lou's fence. You're having an allergic reaction to the scratches from the rose thorns."

"You're something else, Mark," Freddy said, shaking his head. "It takes guts to make an accusation like that when you're all alone in the house."

"What makes you think I'm alone?"

Freddy grinned. "Because I've been parked outside all morning watching. There's nothing to stop me from getting up and breaking your neck."

"You'll be dead before you get out of the chair."

"I'm terrified," Freddy laughed, truly amused. "Do you really expect me to believe you're some sort of geriatric Jackie Chan? You're an old man, sitting in a chair. Unarmed, helpless and, let's face it, rather pathetic. I've killed puppies that were more difficult than you're going to be."

"But I bet they weren't wearing wires," Mark said, lifting up his scrub shirt to reveal the transmitter taped to his stomach. "And they probably weren't backed up by FBI sharpshooters on the roof of the house next door."

Freddy's grin faltered, just a little. "I suppose the house is also surrounded by the French Foreign Legion and a team of highly trained ninjas."

"See that tiny red dot on your chest?"

Freddy glanced down at his chest. There was a tiny pinpoint of red light positioned over his heart.

"That's the laser-sight targeting beam," Mark said. "There's another one right between your eyes. The snipers came up from the beach and took position hours ago."

The Silent Partner raised his head and sat back in his seat, resting his hands on his lap.

"Bravo, Mark. Really splendid work."

Steve came crashing through the front door, gun drawn, followed by Tanis Archer and a half dozen FBI agents, also brandishing their weapons. More agents scrambled up the deck from the beach and spilled into the living room, led by Terry Riordan.

But Freddy seemed oblivious to it all. He didn't even flinch or change his posture as the room filled with cops and FBI agents, all of them training their weapons on him. He remained entirely at ease, as if it was still just him and Mark having a conversation.

"Don't look at me that way, Mark," Freddy said. "You're no different from me."

"I'm not a serial killer, for one thing."

"I didn't think I was, either. I was just like you, Mark. I was fascinated by homicide. I used my profession to get close to it, just like you. Pretty soon, I was killing, too. And I liked it, just like you will."

"I save lives, Freddy," Mark said. "I don't take them."

"For now," Freddy grinned.

Steve had had enough of Freddy Meeks. He yanked Freddy out of his seat, pushed him facedown on the table and pulled his arms behind his back.

"You're under arrest for murder," Steve hissed, handcuffing Freddy and reading him his rights. Freddy looked at Mark the whole time. Mark looked right back at him.

"This is going to make a hell of a book," Freddy said, as Steve dragged him away.

Mark stood up and watched as the Silent Partner took the first steps on his long walk to the gas chamber.

"I'm sure it will," Mark said.

ABOUT THE AUTHOR

Writer/producer **LEE GOLDBERG** is a two-time Edgar Award nominee whose many TV credits include *Diagnosis Murder, Martial Law, Monk, SeaQuest, Spenser: For Hire,* and *Nero Wolfe*. He's also the author of the novels *My Gun Has Bullets, Beyond the Beyond,* and *The Walk,* as well as the non-fiction books *Unsold Television Pilots* and *Successful Television Writing.*

We hope you have enjoyed this Large Print book. Other Thorndike, Wheeler or Chivers Press Large Print books are available at your library or directly from the publishers.

For more information about current and upcoming titles, please call or write, without obligation, to:

Publisher
Thorndike Press
295 Kennedy Memorial Drive
Waterville, ME   04901
Tel. (800) 223-1244

Or visit our Web site at:
www.gale.com/thorndike
www.gale.com/wheeler

OR

Chivers Large Print
published by BBC Audiobooks Ltd
St James House, The Square
Lower Bristol Road
Bath BA2 3SB
England
Tel. +44(0) 800 136919
email: bbcaudiobooks@bbc.co.uk
www.bbcaudiobooks.co.uk

All our Large Print titles are designed for easy reading, and all our books are made to last.